RESISTANCE

DARK ROAD – BOOK THREE

BRUNO MILLER

RESISTANCE:
Dark Road, Book Three

Copyright © 2018 Bruno Miller

Find out when Bruno's next book is coming out. Join his mailing list for release news, sales, and the occasional survival tip. No spam ever.
http://bit.ly/1kkLgHi

Published in the United States of America.

How far would you go for family?

As Ben, Joel, Allie, and their dog Gunner continue their trek across the EMP ravaged country, constant challenges face them at every turn.

The struggle to get through the post-apocalyptic wasteland in an effort to find Allie's dad in Pittsburgh and reunite with Joel's brother and sister in Maryland tests Ben's abilities as a former Army Ranger.

But the teenagers have trials of their own, namely coming to terms with their lost youth as they are forced to grow up fast and make some tough decisions. And as the group passes through one devastated town after another it becomes apparent that only the strong and prepared will survive in these dangerous days.

From kidnappers to roadblocks it seems it's every man for himself in this dangerous new world. Are there any good people left or is this dark road one they have to travel alone?

THE DARK ROAD SERIES

Breakdown

Escape

Resistance

To Mom and Dad
for always encouraging and supporting me
regardless of the adventure

· 1 ·

The dirt road that led back to the main highway seemed a lot shorter than it had last night, but it was still just as bumpy. Joel didn't mind and was glad his dad had decided to let him drive. It felt good to have Allie riding up front with him in his truck, too.

Driving around the wrecks made him a little nervous, though. When his dad had been driving, Joel could look away from them if he wanted to. But now he had to pay attention to each and every one as he drove past, being careful not to run over anything sharp enough to puncture a tire.

He had worked a good part of last summer to save up for a new set of tires for his Blazer. The set that was on the truck when they had bought it wasn't quite up to the challenge of the off-road trails Joel and his friends liked to explore on the weekends.

Having a blowout while four-wheeling was a constant concern, so although expensive, his choice of tire to replace them had been well worth it in his mind. He'd decided on the Goodyear MT/R because they had Kevlar in the tread and sidewall, adding much-needed puncture resistance for off-roading in the San Juan Mountains.

His friend Brian had thought Joel was nuts to spend that kind of money on tires at nearly 260 dollars each. Sure, it was a lot, but the tires were now a year old, and they still looked new.

There was a good chance those pricey tires had saved them from a flat already.

Joel glanced in the rearview mirror. All he could see of his dad was the top of his head, his face hidden behind the large road atlas he was studying. Joel looked to his right. Allie had her window down all the way and her arm hanging out in the air.

He brought his focus back to the road as they came to an intersection. He paused, then turned right onto the main road. There was no point in a complete stop. The highway was empty as usual, and that was good by him.

He checked the fuel gauge. "We have about three-quarters of a tank left."

That brought his dad's head up from the atlas. "We'll start looking for a good place to fuel up when you're down to about a quarter tank. Don't forget we have the two spare cans for backup."

Joel nodded. "I know, but don't we want to save those?"

"We do, if we can." His dad glanced at the atlas again. "The next town looks like it's about 80 miles away. We'll have enough gas to get through, but I think we should find a place to fuel up before we stop, just to be on the safe side. I want to be able to travel a little ways farther once we're on the other side of town, just in case we need to put some distance between us and whatever we run into there."

"Do you think all the towns are going to be so messed up?" Allie looked around the truck for either of them to answer.

"I don't see why not." Joel immediately regretted what he'd said, hoping he didn't sound too pessimistic.

His dad sighed. "As much as I hate to say it, I think Joel is right. People are going to become more and more desperate unless we get into areas that still have services. But who knows? Maybe we're completely wrong and the more populated places are more organized and orderly."

Joel knew his dad didn't believe that for a second and thought he was trying to boost Allie's morale. There was no doubt people would become more desperate as time went on. He was sure Allie knew that, too.

It had only been five days since school had let out for the summer, but to Joel it seemed like another life he'd lived long ago. He couldn't have felt any more removed from being a recently graduated eleventh grader than he did right now.

Did Allie feel the same way? He could only begin to imagine how she was coping, considering her mom was most likely dead. He quickly reminded himself to be thankful for what he had.

He hoped her dad was okay, but based on what she had told him about the man and his skill set— or lack thereof—Joel had his doubts. Pittsburgh was probably in chaos.

They might not even be able to find him. But if they did, what then? Were they just going to leave her there with him and continue on?

Joel didn't want that to happen, either. He might never see Allie again if she stayed there, not to mention he would have serious concerns for her safety. He tried not to think about it and instead focused on the road. No point in worrying about something that hadn't happened yet. Besides, they were a long way from Pittsburgh.

"Look!" Allie pointed through the windshield.

Joel had been so deep in thought and focused on giving the wrecks a wide berth that he failed to notice an old green Chevy Suburban on the road ahead. It was coming at them about a half a mile or so away. They all watched in silence for a minute as it slowly dodged the obstacles on the road.

The Suburban looked a bit like a top-heavy tortoise as it weaved around a pile of cars on one side of the road. The roof was loaded with everything they owned, or at least Joel presumed that by the size of the tarp-covered mound on the roof.

The tarp, which was also green, was tied down with rope that crisscrossed itself multiple times, giving it the odd appearance of a turtle shell from a distance. The unsecured parts of the tarp flapped wildly in the wind. Joel could make out at least two people inside the cabin and thought he saw more but wasn't sure.

"What should I do?" Joel glanced at his Dad, who was now leaning forward between the two seats.

"Nothing yet. Just give him plenty of room to pass." Ben closed the road atlas and tucked it behind him.

Now less than 500 yards away from the newcomers, Joel steered around the last pile of cars between them and the Suburban on the two-lane highway. With nothing else on the road, he could now see the reason for the Suburban's slow approach. The left front wheel had a pretty bad wobble.

"That doesn't look good," Allie said.

"No, not at all. I'm going to say a bent or broken tie rod." Joel had seen a fair number of bent tie rods on the off-road trails back home and knew the death wobble, as he and his friends called it, when they saw it. A tie rod was a pretty common part to damage when off-roading in rocky terrain. When they bought his Blazer, it had a bent tie rod on the passenger side, and it was one of the first things he and his dad fixed together.

"You're probably right about that," Ben agreed.

At a few hundred feet away, the Suburban flashed its lights several times, followed by a waving hand out of the passenger's window.

"They want us to stop, I think." Allie shifted in her seat to face Joel and Ben. "What if they're trying to warn us about something up ahead?"

Joel snorted. "What if they just want our stuff?"

Ben shrugged. "Let's just roll with it and see how it plays out. Allie might be right. It'd be nice to have a heads-up on any surprises down the road. They look like a family just trying to get somewhere like we are."

Allie tucked a strand of hair behind one ear. "And we can warn them about what happened to us and what to expect if they stay on this road."

Even Gunner was sitting up at this point. Roused from his nap by the commotion, he was now straining around Joel's seat to get a better view out the window.

Joel refocused his attention on the Suburban as the distance between them shrunk. He could see and man driving, a woman in the passenger seat, and what looked like a small child in the back seat.

Ben put his hand on Joel's shoulder. "Keep it in gear when you stop. One foot on the gas, one on the brake. Be ready to step on it if you need to. With their wheel wobbling like that, we could lose them fast."

· 2 ·

The loaded-down Suburban stopped first, several yards ahead of them. A man got out with his hands open in front of him, indicating he wasn't holding anything. The woman followed his lead and exited the passenger-side door, waving her hands in the air.

Ben nodded toward the couple as he spoke to Joel. "Leave a good amount of space between us when you stop."

"Okay." Joel turned the wheel to the right and pulled over on the shoulder. That left more than a lane and a half between the two trucks.

The man took a couple cautious steps forward and stopped. "Thanks for not driving past. My name is Jon, and this is my wife, Christine." He repeated his name. "Jon Wilson."

Joel looked over at his dad. "What do you think?"

"So far they seem friendly." Ben was now fully leaned over the center console so he could see out of Joel's window. There was an old faded Air Force sticker on one of the Suburban's side windows.

Joel nodded. "You talk to them, Dad."

"I'm Ben, and this is my son and his friend." Ben tried to answer as vaguely as he could without coming off as rude or aggressive. "Where are you folks headed?"

Jon answered. "Going down to Glendale, Arizona, to Luke Air Force Base, to get up with our son. He's stationed there."

Knowing they were parents of an airman made Ben feel better. "Having some trouble, I see. What year is the truck?"

"Eighty-five, I think. My son left this pretty thing in our yard when he enlisted. He kept promising to come and get it, but now I'm glad he never did. Neither one of our vehicles would run, but this old machine started right up." He jerked his thumb back at the last pile of cars they had passed. "Unfortunately, I wasn't paying attention for a second and ran into one of those."

Ben thought the guy seemed legitimate and his story believable enough, but the pragmatist in him wasn't fully buying it yet.

Just then, a little pony-tailed head popped up from the back window and snuck a peek at them before the mother scolded her for not staying out of sight like her father had asked her to.

Ben nudged Joel. "Go ahead, turn it off and get out, but stay near the truck."

Joel shut the truck off and hopped out.

Ben climbed out after Joel and walked toward Jon with his hand outstretched. "Maybe we can take a look at it and see if there's anything we can do. I've got some basic tools."

"That would be great. We just started having problems a few miles ago." Jon shook Ben's hand and nodded back at the truck. "That was our daughter, Jessie, by the way."

Joel waved. "I'm Joel."

Allie gave a little wave, too. "I'm Allie. Do you mind if I say hi to your daughter?"

"No," Jon said. "She'd probably like that."

Allie headed over to the Suburban's passenger door and introduced herself to Jessie. "Hi, I'm Allie. What's your name?"

"Jessie."

"How old are you, Jessie?" Allie asked.

"I'm nine," she replied.

"It's been a tough couple of days," Christine added in a shaky voice.

"How would you like to come and meet Gunner?" Allie pointed back to the big brown dog who was watching intently from the front driver's seat of their truck.

"Okay." Jessie cracked a smile and climbed out of the Suburban.

Ben looked around, behind the tire that had been wobbling. "Where are you guys coming from?"

"We're from Topeka, Kansas," Jon answered.

"So it took you two days to get here?" Ben asked.

"Unfortunately." Jon shook his head. "And I hate to tell you this, but we drove all night last night, taking turns, which was a mistake in hindsight."

"Why's that?"

Jon looked back at the damaged Suburban. "The wrecks come up fast in the dark." He shrugged.

"I think we can help you guys out. It's at least worth a try," Ben stated.

"Really?" Christine gasped. "That's wonderful!"

"It's a tie rod, like you said, Joel." Ben turned to his son. "It's bent pretty badly, and that's causing the wobble, but I believe we can straighten it out enough to keep you going."

Jon smiled. "I can't thank you enough!"

"Don't get too excited just yet. Let's make sure we can do this. Joel and I have a little bit of experience with these, but not a lot." Ben walked around to the back of the Blazer and started gathering tools for the job.

Jon nodded. "Anything you can do to help us would be great."

"We can show you how to get this one off and then, if you can scavenge a replacement somewhere, you'll know how to do it. You should definitely replace it at some point." Ben handed Joel the Hi-Lift jack and the socket set, then grabbed a hammer and a small crowbar before heading over to the front end of Jon's truck.

Jon joined him there. "I'll get it replaced as soon as I can, but I have a feeling this repair will have to hold us for a while."

"It won't be perfect, but it will be a lot better than it was," Ben said.

"Just let me know how I can help," Jon replied.

"If you have another jack, we should use it as a secondary brace to support the truck since we'll have to do some prying and hammering underneath there. It'll also be a lot easier with that tire off, too."

"I have a jack, and I'll have the tire off in no time." Jon headed around to the back of the Suburban. "It hasn't been easy-going, I'll tell you. Most of the heavily populated areas we've seen have been in total chaos. Early morning seems to be the best time to travel. Where are you guys headed anyway?"

"We're headed all the way to the east coast of Maryland, and by the sounds of it, well, we will be for a while." Ben frowned.

"Whatever you do, mark off Topeka on your map—and Kansas City, too, for that matter—as no-go zones."

"Oh?" Ben listened. This was good information.

"We've seen Topeka firsthand and have heard Kansas City is under mob rule. Supposedly, the National Guard showed up in Kansas City with the intent of distributing supplies through FEMA. We heard they were outnumbered and unprepared for the swarm of people that showed up needing—or should I say demanding—food and water. When they exhausted their supplies, all hell broke loose and things got ugly fast. Rumor has it they were authorized to use deadly force and have done so. It's total guerilla warfare in the city. The Guard pulled out to let the gangs kill each other off."

Ben shook his head. "I had a feeling something like that would happen."

"They're dug in at the downtown airport on the Missouri side of the Kansas River." Jon finished getting his jack in place and began to crank it up to where Joel had already raised the front end of the Suburban slightly. "Okay, my jack is under pressure."

Together, they lifted the truck using both jacks until the wheel was off the ground.

Ben tested the stability of the jacked-up truck by pushing against it with the weight of his body. The truck didn't budge with the two opposing jacks holding strong on either side of the wheel well. Satisfied that the truck was stable, he stepped back and let Jon get to work on the tire. "How did you hear about all this?"

"Our neighbor, good old Mr. Thompson. Really nice guy." Jon looked at his wife and smiled. "He's one of those ham radio guys and a bit a pepper, I guess you call it. God bless him, though. I'll tell you, if it wasn't for him, we'd be in a lot worse shape than we are now."

"There are still some good people out there."

"Thankfully." Jon gave Ben a knowing look before continuing. "Thompson gave us most of his MREs, about six dozen of them, along with a few other supplies for the trip and told us he'd do his best to watch over the house while we were gone. We tried to talk him into coming with us but he wouldn't have it any other way, even after the collecting started." Jon finished up with the tire and yanked it off, letting it roll a couple feet to where it tipped over and came to rest.

"Collecting?" Ben got down on the ground with the socket set and got to work.

Jon was quick to join him under the truck and watched him loosen the nuts at each end of the tie rod. "A group got together and went door to door through the neighborhoods, demanding people give all they had to be divided up among everyone. For the greater good they claimed, but we left before they got around to our part of the neighborhood."

Ben snorted in disgust. "I don't blame you." Jon shook his head. "I never would have thought people would X turn against each other so fast."

"This neighbor of yours, did he hear how all this started?" Ben asked. "We were in the woods on a camping trip when it happened."

Jon lowered his voice as he looked at Ben in the dim light under the truck. "Well, I can tell you what I know, but it's not much, and it's definitely not good."

· 3 ·

Jon cleared his throat softly. "Keep in mind, everything I'm about to tell you has been passed around by a few old-time ham radio guys, so I can't vouch for the accuracy of any of it. There was nothing on the news and no emergency broadcasts prior to the bombs, so nothing official has been said and information has been scarce on the details."

Ben nodded. "Understood."

"From what Mr. Thompson told me, North Korea used nuclear subs positioned off both coasts to launch the ICBMs, enabling them to reach the interior of the country and key cities along the East Coast. They also launched rockets from their bases in North Korea that were able to reach the West Coast."

"Do they know if they were all high-altitude detonations? EMPs? Were there any ground-level detonations?" Ben paused for a second and then got back to using the small pry bar to wedge between

16

the tie rod end and the steering knuckle and hammered it apart before moving on to the inner tie rod end.

"I don't know about that, but I do know that not all the rockets were successful. Some were taken out by our missile defense systems before they reached their targets. But National Missile Defense was down for most of the attack. The North Koreans had help from the Syrians, who set up terrorist cells in the United States and hacked into the NMD."

Ben couldn't think of anything to say and instead focused on getting the tie rod off while he processed all this new information.

Everything Jon said made sense, though, as Ben strung the pieces together in his mind. He'd suspected it was North Korea all along and now remembered reading something a few months ago about the UN accusing the North Koreans of selling supplies to Syria that could be used to manufacture chemical weapons.

They claimed to have evidence and even photographs of known North Korean missile technicians working at Syrian chemical weapon and missile facilities over the last couple years. But like everything else he read or heard about that seemed like important information, there seemed to be no follow-up or consequences by the UN or anyone else. There were trade sanctions, of course, but for a country with a dictator that didn't care about the people, they were useless.

The important issues seemed to get lost, swallowed up or overshadowed by the superficial drivel that passed for news these days. If only the political parties would put as much energy into solving the big issues as they did into digging up dirt on each other and fighting. The only thing any of them seemed interested in doing was creating job security for themselves and maintaining their positions of power. In Ben's opinion, politics had devolved into the equivalent of two kids arguing on the playground. Neither one would listen, and it was all about who could shout the loudest.

Sure, there were a few good politicians, maybe even a handful that hadn't sold out yet, but they weren't the ones getting the headlines and shaping policy. These days, it seemed, that decision was left up to the media and news outlets, which was a whole other issue altogether. They all backed candidates and were partisan without apology at this point.

Ben thought it would be a good idea if politicians had to include a list of campaign donors in their ads. That way you could see what corporations or media outlets were holding the strings. Why did the media seem so hell-bent on pushing society over the edge of decency?

Joel stuck his head under the wheel well. "How's it going, Dad? Need anything?"

"I just about got it." Ben struck the blunt end of the pry bar with the hammer once more, and the tie rod popped off its joint. "There it goes."

He handed the pry bar and hammer up to Joel before he rolled out from under the Suburban. He held the damaged part out in front of him, showing Jon as he joined him from under the truck.

"And that right there is your problem." Ben pointed. "We just need to straighten that out the best we can and then put this back on. Joel, will you get me the ax?"

Laying the tie rod on the pavement, Ben positioned the bent end upward.

"Jon, would you hold that end in place with your foot?"

"Sure."

"I got this end." Joel stepped on the other end of the tie rod.

When they had it secured in place, Ben gave it a few well-placed blows with the flat end of the ax head before picking it up off the ground and inspecting it for straightness.

"I think that's it. Don't want to overdo it and make it any weaker than it already is. Let's get this back on and see how it does."

Ben and Jon crawled back under the truck and went to work reinstalling the tie rod. It went on a lot quicker than it came off.

Jon seemed impressed. "I can't believe how simple that was, or maybe you just made it look easy. I can't thank you guys enough for stopping and giving us a hand." Jon beamed.

Once they had it finished and got the tire remounted, Ben had Jon back the big green Suburban up a good ways and then drive past a few yards so he could watch the tire perform. Jon was already giving Ben a thumbs-up out the window as he rolled by. He quickly brought the Suburban to a stop and parked it.

Christine clapped from the side of the road, where she had been watching Jessie and Allie throw a stick for Gunner. "Yay!"

"That's great! One hundred percent better. You are a life-saver, my friend," Jon exclaimed as he got out of the truck and walked over to Ben. Jon shook his hand excitedly.

Ben accepted the praise without argument. "I still wouldn't go over 40 or 50 miles per hour on that if you can help it. But at least it won't shake you to death. You really should replace it when you can, though. It will give you problems down the road at some point, now that it's been bent."

"We will. I promise." Jon went to stand by his wife.

"Thank you so much!" Christine smiled at Joel and then at Ben. "We can't thank you enough!"

"I wish there was some way we could repay you. Do you want a few MREs?" Jon offered.

"No, thank you." Ben held his hands up. "We have enough food for ourselves. Besides, you have helped us tremendously with the information you gave us. We've been in the dark for so long. At least I feel like I know what's going on now. You're the first people we've talked to since we left Durango yesterday morning. We've had our share of trouble in more than one town on the way, and I would fill you in on the details, but I assume you're going to be taking 25 south, down to Arizona?"

"Yes, we are. We shouldn't be on this road much longer," Jon replied.

"Well, let's just say that's a good thing then and leave it at that. We ran into a lot of trouble in the towns along 160 between here and Durango." Ben glanced at Allie and Jessie, who were sitting in the grass on the side of the road. The girls were busy giving Gunner all of their attention as he hammed it up for them and went through his routine of tricks in exchange for scratches and belly rubs.

"Come on, Jessie," Christine called. "Jessie, come on, sweetie."

"Coming." Jessie reluctantly stood up and made her way over to the truck, but not before giving Gunner a big hug and a kiss on the nose. He reciprocated with a big wet lick on her cheek. She laughed and giggled in the way little girls did, making Ben think of his own little girl for a moment. Then Jessie gave Allie a quick hug before and running back to her mother. She climbed into the back seat of the Suburban and disappeared.

"You guys take care now, and be careful." Ben nodded his goodbye.

Jon and Christine both made their way around to give everyone a handshake and a thank-you before they loaded up in the Suburban. They all waved, even Jessie, who popped back up through the window as they pulled away and headed out.

· 4 ·

"They were nice." Allie was the first to break the silence as they all stood and watched the Suburban disappear down the road.

"Yes, they were. I'm glad we could help them out." Ben walked over to the Blazer and opened the door, letting Gunner hop in first. He glanced at Joel. "You still up for driving? I want to look at the map some more, now that we know a little bit about the roads ahead."

"Sure, no problem," Joel answered.

Ben really was glad that the tie rod repair had gone so well. He felt bad for the Wilsons, especially little Jessie, who reminded him of Emma at that age. Jon seemed nice enough but wasn't really the self-sufficient type. Ben wondered how long he could keep them all safe. Hopefully, they could reunite with their son in Arizona and would be better equipped to deal with things.

Ben was saddened to hear the true state of things, but he was also somewhat relieved to know what they were up against and somewhat encouraged that the military was at least attempting to maintain law and order. If the Guard were in Kansas City, they would be in other places as well and in larger numbers. Maybe by the time Ben and his crew got to Pittsburgh, things would be under control or at least stable enough for them to get in and get out.

He climbed into the Blazer and joined Gunner on the bench seat in the back. "I think the Wilsons might be on to something by going around the towns, even the small ones. We should do the same where we can."

Joel got back behind the wheel and buckled up. "Won't that add a lot of time to the trip, though?"

"It will, but we also need to get there in one piece," Ben stated.

Allie got situated in the passenger seat as Joel started the engine and put the truck in gear. "Sounds good to me, if it means avoiding places that are anything like what we've seen already."

"We'll have to work together. Someone will have to navigate full-time for whoever is driving," Ben said as he looked at the map. He knew picking their way through the back roads using an outdated map would be challenging, to say the least. But based on their recent experiences, it was the option with the least amount of risk involved.

Before long, the rhythmic hum of the engine had replaced the conversation, and even Gunner had fallen asleep with his head on Ben's knee. The dog was half covered under the open map. Sleep tugged at Ben, too, but he rubbed his eyes and struggled to focus on the smaller roads around the upcoming towns.

They were going to have to wing it around some of these places, based on the detail the map provided. Thankfully, the lifted Blazer, with its oversized aggressive tires and four-wheel drive, would allow them to make their own roads where necessary.

Ben also wondered if they should consider changing the hours they were on the road. If they started early, say around four or five in the morning, and stopped by four or five that afternoon, they could use the remaining daylight to secure their campsite and camouflage the truck. Doing that would become more and more important as they made their way east and the population density increased. He was sure the farther they went, the more people they were likely run into.

"What do you think?" Joel asked.

Ben looked up and saw Joel pointing at a gas station coming up on the right.

"We're just about at a quarter tank," Joel added.

"Okay, looks pretty dead around here. Let's do it, but circle around the place once, okay?" Ben looked around and could see at least a couple miles in every direction.

They were well out of the foothills now, and the landscape was changing quickly. Nothing but dry scrub brush and mostly level ground except for the occasional washed-out arroyo or ravine. There was nobody around they could see, and no other buildings, for at least a mile. One small outbuilding sat on the back side of the property, but it looked abandoned.

Joel slowed down and pulled into the gas station. He drove through the parking lot until he completed a loop around the little convenient store. He looked around some more over the top of the steering wheel.

He pointed. "Over there."

He pulled the Blazer over to the tank accesses lids that stuck out partially from the pavement in the corner of the lot. Gunner got up in his seat and began to wag his tail, shifting restlessly and whining a little.

"I think somebody needs to do something," Ben commented.

Joel shut the truck down, and they all got out and stretched their legs for a minute. Now that he was out of the truck and could get a better feel for the place, Ben took a good look around.

The little store here had fared much better than other places they had seen. Some of the windows were cracked, but they were all still intact in their frames. The store itself appeared empty like the others, though, and had obviously been cleaned out by looters. But for the most part, it seemed like a safe place to get fuel and maybe grab something to eat out of the back of the truck while they were stopped.

Gunner quickly found a telephone pole at the corner of the parking lot and relieved himself before he came bounding back to the truck to rejoin the group.

"I wish it was that easy," Allie joked. "Uh, do you think I could use the bathroom here?"

"Joel, how about you unpack the hose and pump and get things ready out here? I'll walk her in and check the place out. When I get back, I can show you how to do it." Ben pulled the tank access key from his pocket and tossed it to Joel. "See if you can figure it out by the time I get back."

· 5 ·

Joel rolled his eyes as he caught the key, then started to unpack the hose. Ben and Allie headed for the store some 20 yards away on the other side of the paved lot.

Ben stopped all of sudden and snapped his fingers, pointing back at the truck. "We're not going to make that mistake again." He jogged over to the driver's side door that was still open and fished around in the center console. A couple seconds later he reappeared with the handheld radios. Turning them both on, he placed one on the rear bumper, then caught back up to Allie.

"Let me know if you see anything." He spoke into the radio and looked back at Joel, who gave him the thumbs-up. Ben clipped the radio to his belt, and they continued on. He wasn't going to get caught off guard again.

It was a little place with only four pump stations out front. "Daisy's Pit Stop" was written in bright yellow letters on the sign over the door. Big round bulbs around the outer edge had once illuminated the sign, but most had been smashed, leaving only the remains sticking out of each socket.

Ben and Allie made their way past the empty shelves and found the bathroom in the back. Ben kept his hand on his gun but left it in the holster as he opened the bathroom door and peeked inside.

He quickly pulled his head out and looked at Allie. "All clear, but I'm afraid it's not much better than the last one."

"I figured." She sighed and pulled her shirt up over her nose.

"I'm going to take a quick look around and then head back out to help Joel. Will you be okay in here alone?"

Allie nodded. "It's fine. Go ahead."

"Here, you keep this then." Ben unclipped the radio from his belt and gave it to her.

"Thanks." Allie headed into the bathroom, still pinching her fingers over her nose through the shirt.

It didn't take long for Ben to look around. The whole store was only about 1,000 square feet with a small storage area in the back—all of which was picked clean, making it easy for him to confirm there was no one else there. Satisfied that he could leave Allie alone in the store, he went out to help Joel.

On his way out, he noticed an overturned shelf with something red sticking out underneath. Pulling at what seemed to be a bag of something, he lifted the shelf a little with his other hand and slid the heavy sack out from under the display. A big bag of dog food.

"Outstanding!" He hoisted the bag onto his shoulder and headed out of the store without giving it another thought.

He was happy with the find. This meant they didn't have to supplement Gunner's meals with their food to make up for the small amount of dog food they had brought with them. He hadn't been able to get to the store before the fishing trip with Joel. He'd been so busy at work he'd figured he would go grocery shopping when they got back. Dog food had been on his list of things they'd needed.

As he exited the store, he could see Joel waiting by the truck and holding the gas cap in one hand and the small silver key in the other. The kid had a crooked smile on his face. Apparently, he had figured out how to unlock the underground tank lid with no trouble.

Ben didn't really like leaving Allie in the store alone, but he also didn't like the idea of the Blazer sitting out front along the highway for any longer than necessary, either. They would only be 20 yards away if she needed them, and she had the radio. He told himself to relax as he walked toward the truck.

"Hey, where's Allie?" Joel asked.

"Still inside. The place was empty except for this." Ben patted the bag of dog food he had balanced on his shoulder.

"Nice find," Joel said.

"Yeah, we needed it."

Joel spun the key on his finger. "Not much of a puzzle."

"Good job. How much fuel have you pumped?" Ben chuckled.

Joel shook his head. "I'm waiting for you. It's all laid out."

"Okay, let me show how this works. It's pretty simple." Ben proceeded to show Joel how to go about setting the pump up and getting the tank topped off without making too much of a mess. As simple as it was, he enjoyed spending some time with Joel doing something trivial for a few minutes.

Once he got Joel started with the hand pump, he let him go and got Gunner's collapsible bowl out and filled it with water. Ben grabbed himself a Cliff Bar out of the back as Gunner began to lap at the water loudly.

"You want anything to eat?" Ben asked.

"Sure." Joel didn't look up from the pump as he cranked the handle around and around.

"Don't wear yourself out there. Pace yourself. It's a marathon, not a sprint." Ben grabbed two more Cliff Bars out of the bag, figuring Allie would want one, too.

He began to wonder when she would finish up and join them back at the truck. He looked at the store, checking for any sign of her, but no Allie yet. He'd give her another minute or two before he started to worry. He didn't want to risk invading her privacy, but his concern was beginning to outweigh that feeling as the minutes ticked by.

"I think it's full. Whoops!" Joel stopped pumping and pulled the short section of hose out of the truck as fuel overflowed from the fill spout. "Crap."

"Pump it in reverse for a bit and get the excess fuel out of the line before you roll it up. That way it won't spill gas everywhere," Ben instructed.

"Okay." Joel did just that and cranked the handle in the opposite direction for a little while until all the fuel was out.

"It's empty now." Ben watched Joel but occasionally glanced back at the store. He fully expected to see Allie walking out any second now.

Joel pulled the long end of the hose out of the underground tank and replaced the locking cap before he rolled the hose up and stuffed it back into the cooler.

"Is Allie feeling okay, or did she say anything to you about being car sick?" Ben looked at Joel.

"No, she hasn't said anything like that to me," Joel replied.

"I wonder what's taking so long. It's been a while." Ben checked his watch and decided he would risk coming off as nosey for the sake of making sure she was all right. He could live with her thinking he was a little overbearing, but he wouldn't be able to live with the fact of something happening to her. "Let's go check on her. How about pulling the truck over to the front of the store?"

"Will do."

Ben turned and began walking toward the store but stopped to call back to Joel. "Don't forget the radio." He pointed to the rear bumper of the truck, where the small walkie-talkie still sat.

"Got it." Joel gave him a thumbs-up.

The Blazer's engine revved to life as Ben neared the store. Joel would be pulling up any second.

Upon entering the store, Ben immediately looked back to the bathroom door before quickly scanning the rest of the place for anything out of the ordinary. The bathroom door was still closed. He went over and rapped on it lightly with his knuckles a few times.

"Allie, you okay in there?" Ben half whispered through the door.

He waited for a second or two but heard nothing. He knocked louder this time.

Boom, boom, boom. The hollow door vibrated like a big drum. Ben's blood pressure shot up. He called out again in a normal voice. "Allie… Allie, are you okay?"

He got nothing again. His brain instinctively kicked into high gear. Just then, the Blazer arrived outside the store.

Joel and Gunner piled out and jogged around the front of the truck before making their way inside.

"She okay?" Joel asked.

Ben shook his head. "She's not answering."

"What do you mean?" Joel said, his voice raised.

"Allie, I'm coming in!" Ben grabbed the door handle and turned it freely. "It's not locked!"

He looked back at Joel for a split-second before focusing his attention on the door. He opened it slowly at first and then flung it wide once his brain accepted the terrible fact that the bathroom was empty.

And Allie was gone.

· 6 ·

"She's gone!" The words came out of Ben's mouth almost before he believed it himself.

"What do you mean?" Joel repeated the question like a broken record, obviously in denial about what he had just heard.

Allie's walkie-talkie was on the floor in the corner of the bathroom. Ben picked it up and looked it over. Allie wouldn't voluntarily leave this behind, which meant wherever she'd gone, it hadn't been of her own free will.

Someone had taken her, although for the time being, Ben kept that thought to himself. No need to scare Joel.

"Here's the radio. She wouldn't have left that. She's here somewhere. There's nowhere else to go for miles in any direction." Ben pulled his gun out and began to give the interior a second look. Had he missed something when he checked the place over earlier?

"I thought you said the place was empty?" Joel asked.

"It was. I looked it over. I didn't see anything or anyone," Ben insisted.

"Where could she be then? It doesn't make any sense." Joel looked around, too. "Dad, check out Gunner."

Ben turned.

Gunner was acting odd and pacing back and forth near the oversized double doors that led to the back storage room. The dog looked at Joel and started to whine.

"What is it, boy?" Joel asked Gunner in a lowered tone.

Gunner sat by the doors the way he would at home if he needed to be let out into the yard.

Ben's eyes narrowed. "I was in that room before when Allie and I came in. It's just an empty room with some built-in shelves. There's nothing in there."

"Gunner disagrees with you." Joel nodded at the doorway. "What do you think?"

"I think it's time for you to get your gun out before we take a look." Ben walked over to the double doors and peeked through one of the two small square glass windows set about head height. He didn't see anything with what little light the lone window on the back wall let in.

That window had been covered with an old sheet turned makeshift curtain, and the filtered light cast the room in a dim yellowish glow.

Ben pushed the left-hand door open slightly and glanced in. He whispered to Joel. "I'll clear left. You clear right."

Joel nodded in agreement.

"Gunner, stay." Ben made eye contact with the dog before he and Joel pushed the doors open simultaneously and went in.

Once inside the room, they could immediately see that they were the only ones there. The room was empty. Unable to resist anymore, Gunner seized the opportunity the wide-open doors offered. He bolted through the opening and into the room.

"Gunner, no," Joel scolded.

"Wait. Let him go." Ben let his door close slowly on the spring-loaded hinge and held onto it until the last couple inches. He followed Gunner over to a black rubber floor mat that was located off to the side.

Gunner sniffed at the mat and followed the edge around with his nose close to the ground.

Now that Gunner had brought the mat to Ben's attention, he thought it looked a little out of place. It was close to the edge of some built-in shelves, and a good part of the mat extended under them.

Gunner seemed unwilling to leave the mat alone and began pawing at the edge, causing it to flip up and then flop right back down when he stopped.

"Help me move this, will you?" Ben motioned to the corner of the mat by Joel's foot as he grabbed the corner closest to him. Together, they dragged the mat several feet backward across the concrete floor.

Joel pointed. "Look!"

Ben was already looking at the roughly three-foot by three-foot trapdoor that was recessed into the floor. The door had hinges at one end and an old rusty clasp that looked like it doubled as a pull handle at the other end.

"Is the truck locked, Joel?" Ben asked quietly.

"I don't think. No, it's not," Joel whispered back.

"How about locking the truck up and grabbing a flashlight or two, then getting back in here before we open this up? If someone took Allie, they could be using her as a diversion to steal the truck. We need to cover our butts here."

Joel swallowed hard and nodded. Ben opened the door he had just closed and held it for Joel. He could see the truck through the empty store. It looked clear. He didn't see anyone around.

"Go ahead, and come right back." He looked at Joel, who hadn't moved yet. "Joel?"

Joel snapped his head up quickly as if he had been in deep thought. "Yeah, sorry. I got it." He started for the door.

Ben thought for a second about having Joel take Gunner and stay at the truck to keep an eye out, but he decided against it, thinking he might need Joel with him for backup. Besides, right now Gunner was the only one that had Allie's trail, and Ben wanted every advantage he could get.

Ben put his hand on Joel's shoulder as he went by, causing him to pause. "Hey, it'll be okay. We'll get her back. We won't stop looking until we do. I promise."

"I know." Joel nodded and put his head down before continuing on to the truck.

Ben knew he was worried; he had every right to be. This wasn't looking good.

But how was Ben supposed to know there was a hidden access under that mat? At least that's what he kept telling himself, but it didn't seem to diminish the guilt he felt over the situation.

He knew better and should have trusted his instincts and stayed with her until she was done. Now she was gone, and it was on him to make it right. Whoever had taken Allie had been lying in wait here for someone to take advantage of, but it wasn't going to be any of them.

Not today.

· 7 ·

Ben kept one eye on the hatch and the other on Joel as he swiftly moved around the truck and made sure it was locked before sprinting back to Ben and through the door he held open.

"How are we going to do this?" Joel huffed.

Ben held his finger up to his lips as he let the door close slowly once again. Getting down on his hands and knees, he put his head near the floor. He pressed his ear to the top of the door hatch and stayed that way for at least a minute.

Joel was getting restless and shuffled around nearby.

Ben held his hand up with his finger in the air, signaling for Joel to be patient just a bit longer. Finally, he sat back on his heels and whispered, "Nothing."

"Do you think she's down there?" Joel asked.

"I don't know, but we're going to find out."

He got his pocket knife out and shimmied it under the edge of the floor hatch, slowly twisting the knife so the hatch lifted. He stopped when there was a gap about a finger's width wide on the leading edge of the hatch, opposite of the hinged side. Then he got down even farther and into a push-up position.

The old laminate floor was cool under his hands as he lowered himself to get a better angle on the small opening he had made in the hatch.

He strained to see, but there wasn't really enough light to make out anything significant. It appeared to be a small empty room with what looked like a pile of rags in one corner. He couldn't see the far side, but he did notice a small amount of light coming from somewhere past what his small opening allowed him to see.

Ben got up off the floor and stood silent for a minute while crouching over with his hands on his knees.

"There's a room down there. I can't see the whole thing, and what I can see, I can barely make out. Get on the other side and we'll lift this hatch slowly."

Ben wanted to avoid using the rusty clasp to pull the door up, thinking the potential for the old metal noisy parts to give them away was too great. With him on the right side and Joel on the left, they wedged their fingers into the small opening.

Each holding their guns in their free hands, they slowly lifted the heavy wooden hatch back on its hinges. The room below was empty in the immediate area under the hatch, and steep wooden steps led down into the space. They continued to lift until the hatch folded back onto the floor.

They laid it down softly, and Ben moved around to the front of the hole in the floor to get a better look at what they were dealing with.

Gunner paced uneasily back and forth at the top of the opening edge, looking down into the darkness.

Ben held out his hand. "Did you bring a flashlight?"

"I got two of them." Joel pulled out two small palm-sized LED flashlights from his back pocket and handed one to his dad.

Ben integrated the light into his two-handed pistol grip before starting his descent into the room. He kept the flashlight off but his thumb on the button, ready to turn it on in a split-second if needed.

He did his best to navigate with the small amount of light the open hatch provided. There was no need to make himself a target with the flashlight any more than necessary. And when it was necessary, it would be quick.

Flash and dash, as he liked to call the technique. He'd use the light in short bursts, only when needed, and move around after he used it so as to not provide the enemy with a trajectory indicator.

Pretty simple stuff really and just plain common sense, he thought, but it was surprising how many people seemed to lose their common sense in a high-stress situation like this and forget the basics.

Ben glanced at Joel before continuing down the stairs. Joel was still up on the floor outside the hatch, waiting for Gunner to move farther down the steps. Ben put his hand out flat in front of Gunner and signaled for him to stay. Gunner sat his back end down on the top step with his front legs still standing on the second tread down, where he waited impatiently.

Ben traversed the last couple steps while his eyes adjusted to the dimly lit space. He could see now that it wasn't a room at all.

It was tunnel entrance.

The tunnel itself was lit by a few weak LEDs strung along a wire that followed the ceiling until it ran out of sight down the passageway. The tunnel must've gone 50 yards before it turned to the left and continued beyond what he could see from the entrance.

Ben looked around the room he was in, his eyes adjusting to the low level of light. In the corner was an old metal folding chair. The chair was open and positioned behind the steps leading down into the dark, musty room. Trash and empty bottles surrounded the chair and littered the corner of the room.

Gunner made it down a few more steps and then jumped the rest of the way, clearing the last few stairs altogether. He immediately began to work his way around the room, letting his nose lead. He stopped at something on the loose dirt floor that caught his interest for a second. Taking in several heavy breaths through his nose, he moved on and wandered a few feet down the small passageway.

There, Gunner stopped and looked back at Joel, who had just stepped off the last stair tread and entered the room. Joel glanced at the tunnel with wide eyes as he headed over to where Gunner had shown interest.

"What'd you find, boy?" Joel bent down and picked something out of the dirt. He stood up and wiped it on his shirt before holding it up to the light trickling in from the room above.

"What is it?" Ben asked.

"Allie's been here!" Joel looked at his dad. "This is a stone from the Rio Grande that I gave Allie last night."

"Are you sure?" Ben raised his eyebrows.

"Positive. I remember the way it's smoothed over and the colors. I'm telling you, this is the one I gave her last night. She had it in her pocket."

"I believe you, Joel."

That was enough to convince Ben that Allie had been taken captive and had been brought down here through this tunnel to God knows where. He hated to leave the truck unmanned, but it was as secure as it could be, and it was tucked in off the road, so it wouldn't be very visible from the main drag.

But none of that really mattered. All that mattered right now was getting to Allie—as fast as they could. If anything happened to her, he wouldn't be able to live with himself.

But first, Ben wanted to make sure they wouldn't be trapped down there. If someone were to close the hatch and lock it while they were exploring the tunnel, they'd be screwed. He didn't want to add "trapped in a hole" to their list of current problems.

"Hang on," he told Joel. Then he ascended the stairs in a few long strides. Once topside he picked the hatch up off the floor. With the one end attached by two brass hinges, he raised the free end until it was at 90 degrees with the floor. He put all his weight behind several powerful yet quiet shoves until the hinges were badly bent. He lowered the hatch and saw that it was no longer lockable, let alone closeable. Then he felt satisfied they were relatively safe from being trapped.

Joel looked at him with a confused look on his face.

"I don't want to get stuck down here. This could all be a setup. You never know. At least we know we can get out that way if we need to," Ben explained.

"Good thinking," Joel said.

"Smart thinking. Always think a few steps ahead and have an exit strategy." Ben used Joel's shoulder for support on his way back down the steep stairway, giving him a little squeeze on the way by and doing his best to project confidence.

Joel nodded as he passed.

"I need you to bring up the rear. You're my eyes and ears. Stay about 10 feet back at all times unless I call you up to me. Got it?"

"Got it."

"Flash and dash, only if you need to. Hopefully these lights run the length of this thing and we won't need our flashlights at all." Ben glanced at the low ceiling before crouching down and heading into the cramped, dark tunnel.

· 8 ·

They followed Gunner down the poorly lit passage, guns at the ready. The tunnel couldn't have been more than five feet high and about the same in width.

To make matters worse, the ceiling had been shored up with wooden planks that were held up with a six-inch timber every 10 feet or so. It was a tight fit and slow going.

Ben didn't like it one bit. They had no idea what they would find up ahead, and he hated how vulnerable he felt stuffed in this tunnel with nowhere to take cover. Best to get through as quick as possible, he thought.

He checked back on Joel occasionally to make sure he was keeping up and staying at a good distance. If he had to back up quickly, he wouldn't be able to go far with Joel right behind him. But Joel was doing as Ben had asked, and he was impressed with the fact that Joel was using the methods they had practiced at the range.

Ben snapped his fingers and got Gunner's attention, who was several feet ahead of him. He held his hand out and pointed down with his index finger, which Gunner knew as the "sit" command. It was one of the few hand gesture commands he and Joel had taught Gunner when he was a puppy. Hand gestures were good for maintaining silence in a duck blind—or, in this case, stalking dirt balls through a secret underground tunnel.

The turn in the tunnel was just a few feet away now. He passed Gunner and slowly peered around the corner, only to see another 20 or 30 yards of tunnel ahead. He motioned for Joel to come up to his position.

"More tunnel ahead, but look." Ben leaned to the side and made room for Joel to peer around the corner.

"See how it gets brighter at the end? And look, we were headed down for a while but now it's angling up. I think we're almost through."

Joel pulled back. "Where do you think it goes?"

"I'm not a hundred percent on this, but I believe it leads to that old outbuilding on the edge of the pavement. We're traveling in that direction."

Joel nodded. "Yeah, I remember that when we drove around the building."

"That's the only other building that's even close to us." Ben wiped sweat off his lip. "That has to be where this goes."

"If that's the end of the tunnel that would be about the right distance between the store and the outbuilding." Joel looked back from where they had come and then around the corner to the section of tunnel ahead again.

"Stay a little closer to me this time, and let's get to the end quickly and quietly." Ben patted his leg with his hand, and Gunner resumed leading the way down the tunnel. They made it to the end pretty quickly, landing at another crude set of steep wooden steps that led up to a large open area above the tunnel exit. Unlike the underground room where they had started, this was more of a hole they were standing in now.

Ben looked straight up. There was a metal roof above them. They were inside the outbuilding. He looked back at Joel and pointed up. Just as he'd suspected.

Suddenly, they heard a noise from the room above. It sounded like Allie's voice, but it was unintelligible and muffled, like she was far away. Without warning, Gunner clawed his way up the nearly perpendicular stairway before Ben could react.

"Gunner, no!" Joel called after the dog, but it was too late. He was up the steps, out of sight, and in the room above them. Ben quickly scaled the rickety steps and stopped just shy of reaching the floor level. He peered over the edge and held his Glock in front of him.

Allie's voice again. This time she sounded excited and more energetic but still muffled. He poked his head up, looked around the interior of the building, and just caught sight of Gunner's tail as it disappeared through a doorway of what looked like a small interior office in the outbuilding.

"Come on, quick!" Ben huffed as he pulled himself out of the stairwell and into the building. Joel was right behind when he rushed into the room after Gunner. The dog was there, and he'd found Allie. The poor kid was tied to a chair, her mouth covered with packing tape.

Ben slowly pulled the tape off of her mouth, not wanting to cause her any more pain, but before he had it halfway off, she took a big breath.

"They're going for the truck!" Allie gasped for air again.

"Get her untied and meet me at the truck," Ben shouted and ran out of the little office, looking for an exit from the building. He found a door quickly but fought the urge to bust through and head for the truck immediately.

"Slow down," he whispered to himself. He steadied his nerves, slowly opened the heavy metal door, and looked out.

Two people were running for the Blazer. It looked like a man and a woman, but he couldn't be sure. The man carried a shotgun and a small bag. The woman was dragging a large bag behind her and struggling to keep up with him. They had already covered more than half the distance between the outbuilding and the backside of the store, where the Blazer was parked.

Once they got to the store and went around the building, he wouldn't be able to see what they were doing, but he was sure they were going to try and steal the truck.

They probably wouldn't be able to get it started, but he didn't want them messing with their stuff or breaking any windows. He didn't feel like driving all the way to Maryland with busted windows.

"Hey," he bellowed. The sound reverberated between the buildings.

The woman glanced back at Ben standing in the doorway, but she quickly turned around and continued on. Now even more frantic, she wrestled with the bag. The man with the shotgun didn't bother looking back, at least not until Ben fired a round from the Glock into the air.

"Stop," Ben yelled again. Now he was standing all the way outside of the outbuilding's doorway, in plain sight of the two runners. The man spun around awkwardly, dropping the bag he was carrying, and brought the shotgun up to his hip.

Ben saw it coming and ducked behind the door, using it as a shield.

"*BOOM… BOOM!*" The shotgun roared to life and echoed off the building.

Ben heard the buckshot more than he felt it as it hit the door he was holding on to. It sounded like heavy rain on an old tin roof as the steel shot ricocheted off the metal-clad building and door.

The first barrage of mini projectiles was followed up immediately by a second round that sprayed the building a little to the right of the door he was behind. Ben was able to get a better look at the shotgun right before he took cover. When the guy spun around to shoot, Ben made out that it was an old double-barrel. At that range, even a 12-gauge shotgun would lack enough power to do any real damage. It would hurt, but it wouldn't be lethal, not to mention the man had just burned through both rounds and would have to reload. Ben wasn't sure if the guy was that stupid or just that desperate.

"Amateurs," he said to himself and shook his head.

Ben had no intention of letting the man reload and capitalize on the moment. He stepped out from behind the door and turned his pistol on the man, who was fumbling around in his pockets for what Ben presumed was more shells.

"I wouldn't do that," Ben advised in a stern voice. He walked toward the couple cautiously.

The woman stopped running and stood motionless after dropping her bag on the ground. She slowly turned to face her partner a few feet away and appeared to be talking to him. She began to make hand gestures toward the man, but Ben couldn't make out what she was saying.

He continued to advance at a steady pace toward their position.

"Drop the gun and get your hands out of your pockets, now!" Ben slowed down a little but kept moving toward the two. The man continued to fumble around in his pockets in spite of Ben's warnings.

The distance between them now was less than 50 yards. The man glanced at Ben once or twice until he eventually pulled two shells out of his coat pocket and frantically tried to load the gun.

Ben was beyond frustrated at this point and losing patience with the situation quickly.

"What's wrong with these people?" he muttered under his breath.

"Don't do that! This is your last warning." Ben repeated his request for compliance as sternly as he could. If the man didn't respond this time, it would leave him no choice.

Suddenly, the woman, her arms outstretched, screamed at her partner. "Please, stop! Just do what he says," she pleaded.

The man stopped moving for a second and looked at her. With a groan, he let the shotgun fall to the ground along with the two shells he had dug out of his pockets.

Ben resumed his approach. "Put your hands up, both of you!"

"We're sorry," the woman sobbed, tears running down her face.

The closer he got, the more he couldn't help but feel sorry for them. They were a filthy mess and looked like they had been living underground or in the old building since the attacks, possibly. Both of their outfits were covered in stains and dirt. The more he looked, the more he began to think they had been living this way for much longer.

Still, though, he had to remind himself that was no reason to do what they had done: kidnapping Allie and attempting to steal their truck, not to mention the man had just fired a gun at him and put all of them in danger. And for what? So that they could steal their truck and supplies?

Not really sure what to do with them, Ben stopped when he was about 20 yards away. He wished Allie and Joel would hurry up and join him. He really just wanted to get out of there, but he felt a sense of responsibility. He couldn't just leave these people here to inflict their brand terrorism on other unsuspecting travelers. That wouldn't be right, and it would weigh heavily on his conscience. What if someone like Jon and Christine and their little girl Jessie had stopped here? Would these people have had any mercy on them, or would they have killed them for their truck and possessions?

Ben knew the answer to that question. It didn't help him in deciding what to do.

· 9 ·

Ben didn't have long to think about anything, though, as he was interrupted by aggressive barking from inside the building, where he'd left Joel and Allie. He knew that bark. It was Gunner's I'm-not-messing-around bark that Ben had witnessed only a few times.

"POP, POP!"

"BOOM!"

The sounds took a second to register in Ben's head. "What the—!?"

He spun around to face the outbuilding, forgetting momentarily about the two would-be thieves in front of him. The sounds of gunfire took precedence, especially as it was coming from the building that the kids were in.

"Joel... Allie," Ben called out. He began to move backward in the direction of the building, trying to keep the two lowlifes at gunpoint.

The man and woman started to back away slowly with their hands in the air at first. Then the man dropped his arms and turned. The woman followed suit and joined in the retreat. They both broke into a run, leaving everything they were carrying scattered on the ground, including the shotgun. Lucky for them, they ran away from the store and the Blazer and headed off in completely different direction.

Ben hesitated for a second.

"Crap," he growled as he spun around. That wasn't how he'd wanted that to go. He sprinted back to the door he'd come out of just minutes ago. Small craters and spots of flaked-off paint, caused by the buckshot, were visible on the steel door and surrounding wall as he approached the entrance.

He glanced back to check on the two runners and make sure they were still headed away and hadn't had a change of heart. He wasn't sure what was going on inside, but he didn't need that clown waiting out here for him with a shotgun. They had made it farther than he'd expected, and he was pleasantly surprised to see them still moving at a good pace away from the building.

Ben opened the door cautiously and made his way into the building, fighting the urge to rush with every move. His heart pounded in his chest. He wasn't sure if it was from the sprint to the door in the hot sun or because of what he was afraid he might find inside the building.

He didn't remember it being this dark in here, but he figured it just felt that way compared to the bright sunlight outside. The only light that penetrated the interior of the old metal building was from a rusted-out spot in the roof. One of the roof panels had begun to give way at the seam where it joined another panel, probably from too many heavy snowfalls. This created a three-foot-long crack a couple inches wide that allowed a dust-filled sliver of sunlight down to the concrete floor.

As his eyes adjusted to the lack of light, he noticed Joel and Allie standing over the hole that led down into the tunnel. Gunner was sitting at the edge and looking down as well. The kid's faces were pale as they stared blankly into the pit.

"Guys, what's going on?" Ben called across the dimly lit warehouse. He stopped, propping open the door with his foot. If the kids were all right, he wanted to keep an eye on the two outside for as long as he could. Then he'd need to get that shotgun secured.

Allie slowly turned to look at Ben. "He had to do it," was all she said before glancing back down in the hole.

Ben wasn't satisfied with that answer at all, and he quickly glanced out the half-open door once more before letting it close behind him.

"What do you mean? Had to do what?" Ben asked as he walked toward them, noticing now that Joel was holding his pistol limply in his hand, both arms hanging motionless at his side.

"He was going to shoot Gunner." Joel shrugged and shook his head slowly. "I didn't have a choice, Dad. It just happened."

"It's okay, buddy. Are you guys all right? Is anyone hurt?" Ben put his hand on Joel's shoulder and then looked at Allie. "Are you okay?"

"We're all fine. Even Gunner." Allie nodded. "He didn't get a shot off until after Joel had…well." Allie paused and shifted her gaze to Joel.

Ben looked over the edge. He saw a body at the bottom of the stairs. It was a younger guy, maybe in his mid-twenties. He was wearing dirty jeans and a blood-stained T-shirt with two bullet holes about a foot apart in his chest. The body was sprawled on the dirt floor. His right hand still clung to a roughly made sawed-off shotgun.

Joel cleared his throat softly. "He came out of the tunnel while I was untying Allie. Gunner started to go crazy, and that's the only reason he wasn't able sneak up on us. By the time I turned around, Gunner had him by the arm and was pulling at him. I saw him start to swing the shotgun from us to Gunner and knew I had to do something." Joel shook as he spoke.

Allie took a ragged breath. "If it wasn't for Gunner... I think that man would have shot us. I was facing the tunnel and saw him. He was pointing the gun at us, but Gunner caught him off guard." She rubbed at her wrists.

"You sure you're okay?" Ben looked at her hands.

"Yeah, just a little rope burn." Allie tried to act casually, but the look in her eyes told a different story. She was freaked out. And understandably so.

With his hands on their shoulders, Ben guided the two back away from the edge of the tunnel entrance. "You did the right thing, Joel. Don't ever question that. It's going to take some time to process that, but right now we need to keep moving." He made eye contact with each of them, trying to bring them back to the present. No doubt they were each reliving what had just happened.

Ben didn't waste any time as he headed down into the hole to retrieve the gun. He wasn't about to leave the shotgun here. It wasn't that he wanted it, but rather that he didn't want the two that had run away to reclaim it when they came back. They might have more guns, but they might not. And if taking this one away prevented them from attacking someone else, he had to do it.

"Keep an eye out at the door for the other two, will you?" Ben asked Joel, hoping that a task would get him firing on all cylinders again.

Joel seemed to come to with a little energy and rushed over to the door. Ben pried the shotgun out of the dead man's grip and hustled back up the stairs.

Allie was waiting for him at the top and launched herself at him with a big hug. She caught him off guard and almost knocked him over with the impact. "Thank you for coming to get me!"

"Whoa!" Ben staggered around Gunner, who had wandered over to get in on the excitement.

"I knew you guys would find me," Allie sobbed. "But I was still scared. I... I didn't know what they were going to do with me." She released Ben from the bear hug and stepped back, wiping her sleeve across her cheeks.

"We weren't leaving here without you, sweetie." Ben gave her a nod and grinned, but he was anxious to keep things moving along and get back to the truck. He headed over to the door that Joel was holding partway open.

"See anything?" Ben looked out over Joel's shoulder.

"No, nothing," Joel replied.

Ben put his hand on Joel's arm. "I'm proud of you," Ben whispered.

Joel didn't say anything, but he nodded as he continued looking out the door.

Ben turned to Allie. "Did you leave the stone on purpose?"

"Yes, I did," Allie replied. "I guess you guys found that?"

"We sure did. That was good thinking on your part." Ben nodded in approval as he pushed the door open and went out ahead of Joel. Stepping out into the afternoon sun, he put his hand up to shade his eyes, squinting as he scanned the horizon for any sign of the other two.

Gunner squeezed out the door, not waiting on Joel and Allie, and immediately started panting when he hit the pavement.

Ben thought it felt hotter than it should have for this time of year. Then he noticed a yellowish haze in the air. Was it like this just a few minutes ago? He couldn't tell if it was smoke or dust, but combined with the heat, it added to the overall feeling of oppression.

There was no breeze at all as they walked across the asphalt parking lot to the truck. Ben was looking forward to getting one of the cold water bottles out from the blanket and could picture in his mind the water droplets sweating on the outside of the container, none of which helped the stale dry feeling in his throat. He was sure they could all use some water, but he wanted to get on the road first.

They needed distance from this place more than they needed a drink.

· 10 ·

They approached the bags and shotgun that were left on the ground. Gunner ran ahead a little and sniffed around the items, pausing every so often at certain spots.

Ben holstered his Glock and was about to hand Joel the dead man's sawed-off shotgun but decided to just to tuck it under his arm instead. Then he bent down and picked up the other shotgun.

He didn't care what they had in the bags, but he wasn't leaving this gun here so they could run their game on some other unfortunate victim. Who knew how many people they had done this to already?

The shotgun looked to be in about the same condition as the other one. The wood looked partially dry rotted with a few missing chunks here and there. There also some severely rusted areas. Both guns had obviously been neglected, to say the least, and were what he would classify as falling into the unsafe-to-shoot category. He was practically doing them a favor by taking these gems off their hands. He would ditch the guns down the road somewhere. The only thing he considered worth keeping were the 12-gauge shells. He had plenty, but a few more wouldn't hurt.

"Want me to carry one?" Allie asked.

Ben was surprised by that after what she had been through.

"Um, sure, if you want." Ben handed her the smaller of the two guns.

Allie held the small shotgun in her hands as she looked it over. "It's heavier than I thought it would be."

"That's a bad example. I wouldn't shoot either of these guns. We're going to ditch them somewhere far away from here." Ben pulled his pistol back out with his free hand as they approached the corner of the store. He couldn't see the truck yet and he wanted to be ready in case there were any more surprises.

He glanced back at Joel to see how he was doing. He hadn't said anything since they left the outbuilding, and Ben was worried about him. "How are you holding up there, bud?"

"Fine," Joel replied, totally devoid of emotion.

Ben knew what that tone really meant, though. It meant Joel didn't want to talk about it, and it was best to let the subject go until he was ready. Ben could respect that, and he understood the need to deal with things internally first.

He remembered his first time taking a life like it was yesterday. That place and time was etched into his mind, never to be forgotten. The difference was, he'd been in uniform and in a foreign country and had known what he was getting into.

Joel was growing up fast, but he was still just a kid in Ben's eyes. It didn't seem all that long ago that he had stood next to Joel, helping him learn how to cast his fly rod. Now he was having to fight for his life in this wasteland of world.

Allie patted her leg. "Gunner, come on, boy. Let's go!" Allie called to Gunner, who was now several feet behind them, still going over the abandoned bags. Reluctantly, Gunner pulled away and galloped toward them, catching up in no time.

Ben held his hand out as he got close to the building. "Wait here a second." He eased his head around the corner. Ben looked into the store, from the large windows out front, to make sure there wasn't anybody hiding inside. "All clear. Come on."

With the kids behind him, he jogged to the truck, where he quickly unlocked it and threw the longer shotgun in the back.

He looked at Allie before he headed around the driver's seat. "Just throw the other gun in the back with that one."

She did as he asked.

"I'll drive for a while. You guys take it easy for a little bit," Ben said as he opened the door.

"Thanks." Allie was already climbing into the back seat with Gunner, who seemed to be happy to be back in the truck and out of the sun.

Joel climbed in next and silently slid into the passenger seat, pulling the door closed behind him. He rolled down the window and leaned out, staring off into the distance.

"We all need to get some water in us. How about getting those cold bottles out when you get situated, Allie?" Ben suggested.

"Sure thing."

He fired up the truck, and the familiar hum of the engine instantly made him feel better. As soon as Joel closed his door, they were moving forward. Ben was anxious to get out of there, but there was one more thing he wanted to do.

He drove out to the edge of the property adjacent to the main road, where a larger version of the sign over the front door stood.

"Hang on just a second. Something I gotta do." He shifted the Blazer into park and left it running as he got out. He made his way to the back of the truck and rooted around in the cooler until he found a can of black paint left over from painting the truck windows. He walked to the large "Daisy's Pit Stop" sign and began to spray-paint a warning to anyone who might come this way.

"Danger! Stay away!" He read it out loud to himself before repeating the message on the other side of the sign. He felt guilty that the two people responsible for kidnapping Allie had gotten away like they did. The least he could do was warn any passersby about what waited here for them.

Even though he had taken their guns, he was sure they would be back at it in no time. Now that one of them had been killed, they would probably be even more ruthless in their tactics. The sign wasn't much, but it was something he felt compelled to do as a decent human being. The can of paint began to sputter as he finished the last letter.

"Good enough," he muttered and headed back to the truck.

"Now we can leave." Ben closed the door and buckled up. Allie looked away from the sign and caught his gaze in the rearview mirror.

"I like it," she said, nodding in approval.

Once Ben got onto the road, he picked up speed and the wind began flowing through the windows. Allie handed out fresh, cold water bottles to everyone. They all drank and sat in silence for a while.

"Oh, by the way, I think I have something that belongs to you." Joel situated himself in his seat so he was turned to face Allie. He dug into his pocket until he pulled out the smooth stone he had given her at the river.

"I'll never let go of this again!" She took the stone from him and held it to her chest with a clenched fist.

The two made small talk for a while as Ben drove. He was glad to see a little life in the boy, and it was good that he was talking with Allie again. It would take a long time for Joel to learn to deal with what had happened, but this was a start.

Between the fresh air and the cool water, Ben was beginning to settle into a more familiar state of mind. And like always in this new world, his thoughts turned to what lay ahead.

· 11 ·

The miles rolled by slowly but surely.

Joel navigated for his dad at every little town they came to, finding alternate routes where they could. Sometimes they ended up several miles off their original route, and sometimes they just skirted the edge of town via the back streets and neighborhoods. Each one resembled the last, with burned-down buildings and houses.

Whatever hadn't been burned to the ground had either been pillaged by looters or fortified and defended by its inhabitants. They passed the occasional pedestrian or small group of people who all had the same thing in common.

It was a look about them—their facial expressions and the way they carried themselves. They were like zombies, lumbering along in search of something. Pale-faced and solemn, they shuffled forward. Some watched the Blazer as it passed by them. Others didn't even acknowledge its existence.

Joel imagined most of them were headed somewhere to reunite with loved ones, or maybe they were just looking for a better place to go.

They had seen a few other vehicles on the road, and while they passed without so much as a wave from the occupants, it was comforting nonetheless. Just to see other cars driving around and a little bit of normal activity made Joel feel better.

Maybe it was the thought that there were other people out there just like them—other *good* people who were struggling just like they were. Maybe it was the thought that they weren't alone or unique in their quest. It was survival of the fittest and the best equipped. Like his dad said, "It was us or them." That was the mentality Joel was resisting. Maybe it was just his way of trying to hang on to his old life.

If he was ever going to see his brother, sister, and mother again, he was going to have to learn to stomach making tough decisions. Clinging to the old life he knew was a waste of energy, and it was beginning to drain him. He found his resistance waning as the days went by and as their distance from home increased. He had to accept that this was their new life and it would never be the same again.

"Well, guys let me be the first one to welcome you to Kansas," Ben joked.

Joel looked out through the windshield and saw the big blue highway sign that read "Welcome to

Kansas" in gold letters with a big sun in the upper corner in the same gold coloring.

"Wow, that's pretty good, right? What time is it?" Allie leaned forward from the back seat, causing Gunner to sit up as well.

Ben nodded. "It's not bad considering all the detours off the main road. It's a quarter to three now. We should probably get gas in about an hour and start thinking about where we're going to spend the night."

"I saw a couple spots on the map that looked like they had some water access. Maybe a good spot to camp. At the rate we're going, I'd guess probably a couple hours away." Joel shrugged.

"I'm good with that as long as it's before I-70. That's all flat open land from there until almost the other side of the state. I want to try to do that all in one day so we don't have to spend the night out in the open." Ben slowed down as they came up to a tight spot in the road.

Joel noticed his dad's facial expression change but wasn't sure what it meant.

Allie exhaled. "Look at that!"

Just ahead of them was an 18-wheeler—or what was left of it. The black skid marks stood out in sharp contrast to the sun-bleached asphalt. It looked like someone had drawn lines on the ground with a giant piece of charcoal. The truck had apparently gone sideways and slid for a while

71

before pitching over and rolling into a pile of twisted metal that covered both sides of the two-lane stretch of highway.

Fortunately, the terrain on either side of the road was relatively flat and open except for a few scrub pine and sandhill sage bushes.

Joel gawked at the scene "What a mess."

Ben steered them across the oncoming traffic lane and down off the road, giving the accident a wide berth. The Blazer easily clawed its way over the rocks and bushes as they made their own detour.

Joel wasn't sure if he noticed the vultures or the horrifically pungent smell of rotting meat first, but it was enough to make him gag instantly.

"Oh man. That's bad." Joel yanked his shirt over his nose.

"That was a refrigerated truck." Ben pulled his shirt over his nose as well.

Joel looked back at Allie, who had done the same by now. Gunner was the only one who didn't seem bothered by the nauseating smell the warm breeze was blowing in their direction. Joel was pretty sure he could hear the flies buzzing from one water-stained crumpled box to the other. They were scattered all over the road and looked like they had thawed long ago and were well along into decay.

Vultures had torn most of the boxes open and scattered the contents. The large black scavengers ignored the truck as it drove by, too busy squabbling among themselves over the putrid meat. The vultures that did take notice of them were in the groups on the outskirts of the feeding frenzy. They refused to move out of the way forcing them to drive even further around the accident. Joel noticed a few of them actually lunged at the Blazers tires with their sharp beaks.

"Do you see that? Their attacking the tires. That's crazy!" Joel leaned out the window and looked down at the birds.

"Why would they do that? Do you think they could hurt the truck?" Allie asked.

"I don't know but let's not find out." Ben honked the horn in an effort to scare off the large aggressive birds.

As they cleared the last group of vultures Ben steered the blazer around the front of the wrecked semi and began to climb back up the shoulder of the road, the wind switched directions and the smell dissipated. Joel lowered his shirt and took a small breath through his nose, sampling the air.

"It's gone," he said, breathing in deeply. But the assault on his senses was far from over. Just as Joel was feeling grateful for the fresh air, he saw something he would never forget.

The driver's body was sticking out of the shattered windshield, frozen in the agony of the moment. The arms remained outstretched as if he were still trying to fight off the ravenous vultures who were, no doubt, responsible for nearly picking his carcass down to the bone. Very little skin remained, and what did looked baked to leather by the relentless summer sun. The mouth was wide open, telling a tale of what must have been terrifying last moments.

Joel tried to look away but felt unable to react until he had already seen more than he wanted. He closed his eyes and took a deep breath, trying hard to put the image out of his mind and trying to forget the smell. But they seemed intertwined and he couldn't shake it. He couldn't fight the urge in his gut any longer and had no other choice but to give in.

He hauled himself out the window and threw up. He felt a hand on his back as he involuntary dry heaved repeatedly. The convulsions finally subsided, and he was able to compose himself and sit back in his seat.

From the back, Allie handed him a paper towel to clean up. He was embarrassed about what had happened but quickly forgot all about it when he realized it was her hand on his shoulder. He still felt a little dizzy and took a sip of water before leaning back in the seat and closing his eyes.

"You gonna be okay? Need to stop?" his dad asked.

"No, I'm good. Keep going," Joel answered but kept his eyes closed and his head back. He could feel the truck had returned to the smooth pavement again and tried to imagine they were far away from the wreck.

With a fresh breeze now moving over them once more and Allie gently rubbing his shoulder, he had no trouble drifting off to sleep.

· 12 ·

"Hey, Joel! Hey, buddy!" Ben tapped Joel's shoulder lightly, trying to wake him up.

"Huh, what?" Joel squinted and rubbed his face.

"We need to stop for gas soon." Ben scanned the horizon ahead. He hadn't seen a viable station in miles, but there had to be one soon.

"Sorry, I fell asleep." Joel straightened up in his seat.

"It's okay. You needed it. Allie has been helping me navigate."

Allie patted his arm. "We're looking for a place to stop now. You were asleep for over an hour." She moved over on the bench seat to just behind the center console. She practically had the whole seat to herself.

Gunner was all the way over to one side behind Ben's seat. He had wedged himself in between the seat and the truck frame and positioned his head to take full advantage of the wind blowing in the driver's side window. He practically had his head on Ben's shoulder.

"Want me to get him back here with me?" Allie asked.

"No, he's fine." Ben gave Gunner a brisk rub behind his ears.

They rode on for another 15 minutes or so until Joel spotted a place up ahead.

"How about that place?" He pointed.

Ben slowed down as they approached so they could get a better look at it before they committed to getting off the road.

After what they had just been through, he wouldn't stop if he saw anything out of place. They had the spare cans of fuel in the back if they needed them and could afford to wait for the right place to stop if it meant less risk.

The Shell station was more modern than the last place they'd stopped, and now that they were drawing closer to the plains, it was surrounded in all directions by agricultural land, mostly used for raising free-range cattle. Not that there were any visible.

He had noticed the lack of livestock in their travels but hadn't said anything about it to the kids. He figured any rancher worth his salt would have rounded up the herd and brought it in close to the ranch. A Black Angus bull would probably be worth its weight in gold right now with the dwindling resources. Ben imagined the ranchers were going to have their hands full protecting their livestock when the food ran out.

"Look's empty." Joel sat back in his seat, allowing his dad to see out his window as well.

Ben raised his eyebrows at Joel. "Yeah, so did the last place."

"Well, don't worry about me. I won't be going inside," Allie promised.

"Sounds like a plan." Ben finally brought the truck to a stop on the shoulder, just in front of the Shell station. He sat and scrutinized the place, trying to play devil's advocate to find a reason not to stop here, but he couldn't. They needed fuel, and this place would be no different than the next one.

He pulled into the parking lot and quickly found the underground fuel storage fill pipes sticking above the asphalt.

"How about we have the AR handy?" Ben looked at Joel.

"Got it!" Joel began to get the gun out of the bag as Ben parked the truck and shut the engine off.

Gunner jumped over the console and followed Ben out the driver's door, while Joel helped Allie out on the other side. As soon as Gunner hit the ground, he was off like a shot, tearing around the parking lot like he was possessed.

"I think somebody has a little energy to burn!" Allie laughed at Gunner's crazy display. "But I get it. It feels so good to stretch." She pushed her arms out in front of her as she watched Gunner run around in circles.

Ben nodded. "We could all use a break soon. Another hour or so and we'll start looking for a place near where you saw water on the map. We have enough to get by, but it would be nice to have access to a river or even a stream. I wouldn't mind changing clothes and washing what I have on. It would be good for morale." It was going on a week since any of them had bathed.

"Sounds good to me." Joel slung the gun over his shoulder. He wandered to the front of the truck, where he could see down the road in both directions for quite a ways.

Allie followed him around front while Gunner moved on to a more casual search of the grounds. She gave Joel an excited smile. "Your dad said he would teach me how to use you your 20-gauge shotgun."

"Nice." Joel nodded and looked back at his dad. "When are you going to do that?"

"Tomorrow morning after we break camp. I figured we would get her familiar with your Weatherby and that little .38 from the store. They're both good guns for her to start with, and she needs to know how to protect herself, should the need arise."

"It was my idea," Allie said, putting her shoulders back.

That made Joel grin.

"Okay, who wants a little exercise?" Ben stepped back from the hand pump as he finished getting it all set up.

"I'll do it." Joel pushed off the truck fender where he was leaning, walked over to his dad, and handed him the AR.

"Thanks." Ben patted him on the shoulder and walked to the front of the truck, where Allie was watching Gunner.

"I wish I had his energy." Ben shook his head as Gunner checked every nook and cranny in the small parking lot with his nose.

"He really saved our butts back there." Allie looked off into the distance.

Ben could tell she was trying to maintain her composure. She hadn't offered any details about how they'd captured her or how it had gone down, and Ben didn't want to pry. If she wanted to talk about it, she could when she was ready. It didn't matter anyway. It was over and she was safe.

"I'm sorry Joel had to do that because of me. I feel like it's my fault," Allie blurted out, checking in Joel's direction as she lowered her voice. "I feel so bad that I caused all that trouble."

"Don't ever feel that way, not for one second. Nothing that happened back there is anyone's fault except the three people that caused it." Ben looked at Allie. "We're all in this together, and we'll take care of each other."

She nodded, the serious tone in her voice extending to the look in her eyes. "That's why I want to learn how to use a gun."

· 13 ·

Joel finished the fueling process and cleaned up while Ben and Allie talked and kept watch at the front of the truck.

"Just about finished," Joel called out.

"Good," Ben answered.

"Here, Gunner, get some water." Allie poured the rest of her water bottle into Gunner's collapsible orange dog bowl. He eagerly lapped up the water, taking a break to breathe only once before the bowl was empty. Then he stood over the empty bowl and panted as he looked up at Allie.

"He certainly has taken to you." Ben smiled as he headed back around to the driver's side door.

"He's my buddy, aren't you, boy?" Allie said in a silly voice and gave Gunner a hug before she coaxed him up into the truck.

Ben hesitated for a moment before he got in. He called back to Joel. "You got it?"

"Yep!" Joel finished up and stuffed the gloves under a bungee strap, then turned to look at his dad. "Did you bring my shotgun?"

"Yeah, it's in the truck," Ben answered, remembering he hadn't told Joel about the modifications he had made to the gun.

"Huh. I didn't see it when we were loading. Are you sure?" Joel asked.

"Oh yeah, it's in there. I, uh, well, I made a few small modifications to it so you probably didn't notice it." Ben got in the truck and pulled the door shut.

"Modifications? Would you like to explain what that means?" Joel hopped up into the passenger seat.

"I just made it a little more compact." Ben shrugged, purposefully teasing Joel with his vagueness.

"Where is it?" Joel asked.

"Allie, under your seat you'll find something wrapped in an old gray towel. Would you hand that to Joel, please?" Ben asked as he started the truck and put it in gear.

Allie reached under the seat and felt around for a few seconds, then maneuvered the towel out from under the seat. Gunner's curious nose gave the bundle a good sniff as Allie passed it up to Joel.

"This is my shotgun?" Joel laid it on his lap and unrolled the towel, revealing his 20-gauge

Weatherby. "Or at least what was left of it." Joel sat in silence for a minute as he examined the weapon.

Ben noticed Joel's attempt to hide the grin forming on his face.

"That's pretty cool actually," Joel remarked.

"Is that the gun I'm going to learn how to shoot?" Allie asked.

Ben nodded. "That's one of them."

"I like the camo color. It's pretty," Allie joked.

"You did not just call my gun 'pretty.'" Joel shook his head and began to go over the mechanics of the shotgun with Allie.

Ben was glad to see the kids joking around again and making small talk. This was the first time both of them seemed to totally forget what they had just been through. At least Ben hoped they could forget about it for a little while. They were doing remarkably well for two teenagers who just had their lives turned upside down.

He had noticed a lot of distant stares from them, like they were deep in thought, but he was sure they could say the same about him. So much change in just a week's time and so much to come to terms with.

"How about taking a look at the map and finding us a spot to call home tonight?" Ben hated to interrupt their conversation, but he had just seen the sign for Oakley, Kansas.

The landscape around them was changing quickly and he knew that meant they were getting close to I-70. From what he remembered of that area, after Oakley, there wasn't really anything to speak of for hundreds of miles—nothing but agricultural land as far as the eye could see.

The vast open spaces and fields of windswept grain weren't bad scenery, but at this point in June, most of the wheat would have probably been harvested, leaving only barren dry fields and wheat stubble with little cover or resources to be had. They would stick out like a sore thumb among the landscape.

He was hoping the isolation and lower population of this area would also mean more open sections of road and fewer wrecks. They needed to find a place to stop before they got on I-70. Then they could get an early start again tomorrow and hopefully make it to Missouri by day's end.

But that all depended how long it took to get around Topeka and Kansas City, two places Ben planned on giving a wide berth. After the information Jon had given him, he had decided to avoid those places, but what they had recently been through had solidified that decision even more. He resisted at first, thinking that it would add too much time, but now he realized if they didn't, they most likely wouldn't make it at all.

If they maintained this rate of travel, he figured they could be there in about a week's time, but he hated to speculate that far ahead without knowing what challenges still lay ahead.

Besides, they had to get into Pittsburgh still, and that alone could take time. He had been giving that some thought and was leaning toward leaving the truck outside the city and hiking in. Going on foot would add a lot of time, but Pittsburgh was a big city. The situation there could be the same as what Jon described in Kansas City.

At least by the time they got close to Pittsburgh they would be into the Appalachian Mountains. Late June in the Appalachians would be a resource-rich environment. The weather for camping should be pleasant with plenty of cover to keep them out of sight. He was sure they could find somewhere around Pittsburgh to hide the truck.

When he'd packed the final few things in the Blazer, he'd thrown in an old piece of camouflage netting that he and Joel had used for making hunting blinds. He wasn't sure what they would do with it until now. The netting was easily large enough to cover the truck.

Pittsburgh was probably at least a couple days away, but Ben knew it was never too early to start planning, especially when the stakes were this high.

· 14 ·

"Based on that sign back there, we should see water of some kind in the next few miles. Look for a bridge." Joel pitched forward in his seat, scanning the road ahead.

"It's hard to tell." Allie leaned over his shoulder and looked at the map.

"Yeah, it doesn't really show much on here but a thin blue line." Joel pointed.

"There's something coming up." Ben sat up in his seat a little higher. He saw a small bridge over two large culvert pipes. The closer they got, the more the waterway looked like an irrigation canal.

Ben spotted a dirt road off to the right and decided to take it. An irrigation ditch would have to do tonight. There would be no fresh-caught trout for dinner, but at least they would have a water source.

They stayed on the dirt road that followed the ditch for a couple miles before it turned off toward the east. There was a large pump house there for the irrigation system, and Ben pulled the truck in behind it as best he could. They were far enough off the main road that he doubted anyone could see them, but just the same, he didn't want the silhouette of the Blazer visible.

Ben got out of the truck and felt the short dry wheat stubble crush under his feet. Of course, Gunner was out next and didn't let the fact that Ben wasn't completely out of the way stop him from squeezing by. He didn't waste any time and got right to exploring their new campsite.

"It's so empty out here." Joel looked around as he held the door open for Allie until she was out of the truck.

"It is," Ben answered.

Other than the distant irrigation systems that sprung up every so often on the horizon, there was nothing else around for as far as they could see. The water flowed in the ditch at a pretty good rate and seemed clean. It would be easy work for the filters, and they could clean up their dirty things and take plenty of fresh water with them in the morning.

It was a little earlier in the evening than when they had stopped last night, so there was plenty of light left to get things done.

"I'll wash the clothes for us," Allie offered.

"I'll give you a hand," Joel added.

After they had all cleaned up and changed, the kids sat by the side of the ditch and worked on the clothing with a bar of soap while Gunner watched and chased a few soap bubbles down current.

Ben wished there were more resources here. There wasn't enough material around to start a fire, let alone keep one going long enough to cook dinner. Thankful to have the gas stoves and fuel, he began to sort through the dehydrated food pouches.

"What's for dinner?" Joel called out.

"Southwest beans and rice." Ben held up three pouches from the back of the truck.

"Well, I'm glad Gunner is sleeping with you tonight!" Joel looked at Allie and snickered.

"Oh, thanks." She smiled.

"Fortunately for all of us, I found a bag of dog food a few stops back, so Gunner can get back on a semi-normal diet. And we can all breathe a little easier," Ben added.

"Awe, poor Gunner. We still love you, stinky boy." Allie patted Gunner on the head with a wet soapy hand as he licked at her fingers.

Ben set up one of the stoves and got a pot of water going. While he waited, he strung a section of cordage from the pump house to one of the load bars on the roof rack, making a place for Joel and Allie to hang the wet clothes.

He looked up at the sky. The light was noticeably fading, and he thought for the first time in a while the sky looked close to normal. No haze, no plumes of smoke. He couldn't help but wonder if that was because of their location.

If North Korea had launched attacks from both coasts, maybe the middle of the country was out of reach and isolated enough to be spared the full impact from the EMPs. Still, though, he hadn't had any luck picking up a signal with the radio today and was beginning to think he never would.

But he would try again tomorrow, and he would continue to try until he got a signal. If Jon's neighbor in Topeka could communicate with his ham radio, then people were still broadcasting. They just weren't close enough to pick up the signal with their weaker handheld units.

The water began to boil. Ben turned the stove off.

"Dinner in about 15 minutes." He called over to Joel and Allie, who were starting to hang some of the clothing up to dry. A coyote howled off in the distance, and he was reminded about the run-in he and Gunner had the other night.

He grabbed the small folding shovel off the rack and locked the blade in place before he stuck it into the dirt near the stove. "We better clean up pretty good tonight after dinner. We don't want any guests in camp tonight. We'll bury the trash before we go to bed."

Allie chewed her bottom lip. "Will they bother us?"

"No, they shouldn't. We won't give them a reason to stop here. We just need to put everything away that might interest them."

"Okay." She swallowed.

Joel put his hand on her shoulder. "It'll be all right. You'll have Gunner with you anyway."

"Come and get it." Ben called them over to eat and handed them each a pouch of food with the top still folded down to keep the heat in.

"Thanks," Allie said.

Joel followed her over. "Yeah, thanks, Dad."

"Yep, enjoy." Ben walked to the truck and took a seat on the open tailgate, where he had the map laid out. He unfolded his meal pouch and set it down, letting it cool for a minute before he attempted to eat the steaming hot contents.

Gunner followed the kids to the edge of the irrigation ditch, where they took a seat in the grass. He found a spot between them and lay down, knowing it was too soon to beg for leftovers yet.

Ben watched them for a moment and thought about how he had wasted time stressing over bringing Allie with them in the beginning. He couldn't imagine it any other way now and could see what a huge morale booster it was for Joel to have her along. He certainly had seen a change in Joel, for the better, over the course of the last week.

It was hard to believe he was the same kid who had to be reminded to take the trash out.

A person could take a tragedy like this in one of two ways. They could either adapt and survive or let this new world beat them down. And it appeared that both Joel and Allie were adapting well. He was glad they had risen to the challenges that had been thrown at them. Otherwise, this would have been a much different trip.

Pride in his son overwhelmed him right now. He could see that all the things he had tried to teach Joel over the years hadn't fallen on deaf ears. Ben was thankful to be blessed with such a remarkable son.

Allie seemed like a special girl as well. She was clearly a fighter and wasn't afraid to get her hands dirty. He could see why his son was attracted to her. She had been through a lot these past few days, and today was no exception. Yet here she was, several hours later, laughing with Joel as they ate their dinner. Even Gunner had accepted her immediately, and that was something he didn't do with too many people.

If they managed to find her dad in Pittsburgh, it would be tough to leave her there with him. Ben also worried about Joel and how he would take it. It would be hard on him to lose Allie. The bond developing between them was easy to see. Ben would have to be blind not to notice the way they looked at each other. It was only natural and probably a good thing, considering the current state. At least they had that one positive distraction from the horrors they had to endure.

He would definitely have to teach Allie how to use the shotgun and the .38 pistol. If they were going to leave her in Pittsburgh, they could at least give her a fighting chance to take care of herself and her dad.

· 15 ·

After dinner everybody squeezed out the remains of their pouches on top of the dog food in Gunner's bowl. Gunner hurried over to see what he had scored. He looked back at them when he saw the measly leavings in his bowl.

"That's it, boy! We were all hungry tonight. You have plenty of dog food in there." Joel shrugged and headed to the truck to grab the gear. As Gunner ate, they cleaned up from dinner and set the tents up. Joel dug a hole for the empty food bags, then buried them about a foot underground in the hard, dry dirt.

"That ought to do it." Joel smiled at Allie.

They hadn't heard the coyotes in a while, and Joel decided not to say anything more about it. He didn't want Allie to worry unnecessarily. Joel and his dad had camped around coyotes plenty of times and never had any trouble. In fact, it was pretty common to hear them call back and forth to each other as the sun went down. But that must have been a fluke the other night at their house. He'd never heard about them being aggressive like that before.

A part of him wondered if the EMPs had changed some electromagnetic fields or in some way had an effect on the animals. He'd heard about animals having a sixth sense about things like that. Joel remembered his teacher in science class talking about how scientists had found that animals and insects were able to sense electromagnetic energy and electromagnetic fields.

They'd read in their textbooks that birds used the Earth's electromagnetic field to follow migration routes, how bears timed their hibernation by it, foxes used it to hunt, and so on. If animals used electromagnetic fields, maybe a disturbance would throw them off or make them more unpredictable at the very least.

How could explosions of the size they'd seen not have an impact? If he thought about it long enough, Joel could still feel the impact of the detonations that fateful morning. He would never forget how small he felt standing in the woods in the middle of nowhere as the shockwave rolled over them.

Joel thought back to the overturned truck earlier in the day and remembered how aggressive the vultures had seemed. Was that normal? He had no idea. What did he know about vultures? Nothing, that's what. Then he remembered the half-eaten remains of the truck driver hanging out of the smashed front window and forced himself to think of something else. Anything else. He was getting carried away with his ridiculous theory about crazy animals.

Joel threw his sleeping bag into his tent and headed over to the irrigation ditch with the water pump and empty bottles.

"Need some help?" Allie asked as she finished unrolling her sleeping bag and zipping her tent flap closed.

"Sure." Joel paused to wait for her and was soon joined by her and Gunner. His dad was still studying the map with the red light of his headlamp. Gunner beat them to the ditch and washed his dinner down with large gulps of fresh water before rolling in some tall grass.

"What are you doing, dog?" Joel laughed.

Gunner paused briefly before resuming his antics in the grass. Allie and Joel sat down at the edge and filled the water bottles. Joel pumped the handle on the filter and Allie switched the bottles out and capped off the recently filled ones. She placed them in a row along the edge of the ditch, and before long, they had them all done.

"What are you going to do when we get to Pittsburgh and find your dad?" Joel asked.

"You mean *if* we find my dad. I'm beginning to wonder if I'll ever see either of my parents again." Allie looked down at a piece of grass she was twirling around her finger.

Joel put his hand on Allie's knee. "If he's there, my dad will find him."

"I hope you're right. If not, I guess you're stuck with me." She laughed nervously and forced a smile.

"That would be okay with me." Joel tried his best to sound encouraging, but he knew the reality of it just the same as she did. She had mentioned that her dad was an IT guy and pretty much a stereotypical city dweller. He lived in an apartment building close to the center of the city. Based on what they had seen and heard, the more populated the areas, the worse they seemed to be.

It only stood to reason that Pittsburgh would be no different. Joel had his doubts that they would find Allie's dad. And if they did, would he be okay? He might be hurt. Or worse.

What if they did find her dad, though, and he was fine? Did that mean that Allie would stay in Pittsburgh? Her dad couldn't take care of her the way they could.

Joel didn't want her to stay in Pittsburgh. The more he got to know her, the more he liked her. And he couldn't bear the thought of continuing on without her. He knew that was selfish, though, and didn't dare let Allie know how he felt. She had already lost her mom, and he couldn't imagine the anxiety she was coping with, not knowing if her dad was okay.

It was easier to talk about something else and avoid the topic altogether. Every time he thought about her loss, he realized how lucky he was to have his dad and at least the hope he would see his mom and siblings again. Honestly, he wasn't sure how Allie was keeping it together. Compared to his situation, her outlook seemed bleak.

At least Pittsburgh was still a couple days away, but it was something they would have to deal with soon enough. Joel was sorry he had brought it up.

"So you're going to learn how to shoot, huh?" Joel asked in an attempt to change the mood.

Allie looked up from her thoughts. "Your dad thinks it's a good idea, and so do I. From what I've seen, it couldn't hurt to know how to handle a gun."

"Well, I think it's a good idea, too." Joel smiled.

"You're lucky your dad taught you all this stuff." Allie glanced around at the tents.

"I never thought I would put it to use like this, though." Joel unscrewed the last bottle from the filter and put the lid on before standing. "Have you ever shot a gun before?"

"No, never even held one before." She gathered the last three bottles.

"There's nothing to it." Joel reached out his hand to Allie and helped her off the ground.

They made the short walk back to the truck, where Ben was just shutting the cover of the atlas.

Ben nodded at the bottles. "Thanks for taking care of the water, guys."

"Yep," Joel answered.

"You're welcome." Allie smiled.

Joel spotted the atlas on the tailgate. "What's the plan for tomorrow?"

"Let's try to get an early start, like 4:00 a.m. early. Maybe after the sun comes up we can find a place to stop. We'll look for a remote spot where Allie can practice shooting and we can have breakfast." Ben checked his watch and then turned off his headlamp.

"Sounds good," Joel said.

Ben hopped off the tailgate. "I'm really hoping once we hit I-70 things will open up and we can make up for lost time."

"How far do you think we'll get tomorrow?" Allie asked.

"With a little luck, I don't see why we couldn't make it halfway through the state of Illinois and maybe on to Pittsburgh by the next day." Ben shrugged.

"Wow, really?" Allie's eyes widened.

"Maybe Maryland the day after that. Maybe. A lot can happen between here and there." Ben looked at Joel, then back at Allie.

"Yeah," Joel said. "But still, in the next few days we could be there and get Brad and Emma and Mom!"

"Possibly, yes. But that means getting some rest tonight so we can have a productive day tomorrow. If the road does open up for us tomorrow and we can make better time, which means lots of fuel stops. And on that note, I'm going to hit the rack." Ben tossed the road atlas onto the back seat and closed the tailgate. "I'll have coffee ready at four. Good night, guys." Ben turned and headed to his tent.

"Love you, Dad," Joel said.

"Love you, too, bud."

"Goodnight," Allie answered.

They all turned in for the night and were asleep before long. Tomorrow would be another long day filled with unknowns. The more rest they had, the better prepared they would be—and the better chance they'd have for survival.

· 16 ·

Allie awoke with a start from a deep sleep to the sounds of the stove being set up somewhere outside her tent. Gunner, who had slept in the tent with her, whined at the zippered flap to be let outside.

"Hang on." Allie opened her sleeping bag just enough to get her arm out and fumbled with the zipper on the tent. She barely had it open when Gunner forced his way through the small hole.

She peeked through the opening. Joel and his dad were at the back of the truck, setting up the stove and talking. She lay back down for a minute and stared at the tent ceiling, noticing the crisscross weave pattern of the orange material as her eyes adjusted.

She wanted to relish the warmth of the sleeping bag for just a few moments longer before she got up and faced the cool dampness of the morning. The temptation to linger there in her bag was strong. She could have easily drifted back to sleep. But as much as she wanted to continue lying there, she knew that it was time to get up, and she didn't want to be the reason they were late getting started today.

She got dressed and pulled her fleece on before she unzipped the tent flap the rest of the way. She put her shoes on and slowly got up and stretched. It still felt like the middle of the night to her, and for all she knew, it could be.

"Good morning!" Joel headed in her direction, holding two steaming cups of coffee in his hands.

"Oh, thank you! Good morning." Allie smiled as he handed her one of the cups. Ben was already packing the stove and the coffee pot away in the back of the truck. She was glad she had pushed herself to get moving and join them.

She wasn't sure what felt better: drinking the coffee or holding the warm cup between her hands. She didn't remember it feeling so chilly last night. Maybe it was the dampness or maybe she was just tired. She didn't sleep well last night and woke up several times with bad dreams. Nothing she could remember specifically, but they kept her up off and on all night.

"What time is it?" she asked.

"A little after four," Joel answered.

"Oh. So that's why I feel like this," she joked.

"Yeah, it's pretty early," Joel said. "This is about the time we get up when we're going on a hunting or fishing trip, and this is our typical Saturday morning in the winter. Gunner's already in the truck. He thinks we're going hunting or something." Joel looked back at the truck and shook his head.

Allie could see Gunner sitting up in the front seat and panting with way too much excitement for this early in the morning.

"You guys are nuts. I think Gunner and your dad are on the same vitamins." Allie laughed as she watched Ben tidy up and break down his tent with energy that shouldn't have been possible at this hour.

"Yeah, we should probably get our gear packed up, too." Joel glanced at his still-standing tent.

"You're right," Allie agreed and reluctantly set her coffee down after taking one more quick sip.

They both got to work rolling up sleeping bags and collapsing tents, and before long, they were handing their gear up to Ben, who stashed it away neatly in the rooftop carrier.

Ben closed the lid on the cargo box and locked it before getting in. "Let's hit the road. You guys ready?"

"Ready," Joel replied.

"Ready, too," Allie said as they headed around to the other side of the truck and started to get in.

Ben stopped them. "Hey, Joel, how about sitting in the back seat so you can get to the ammo cans in the back? I want you to get the .38 and the shotgun ready for Allie. I think the 20-gauge shells and the bullets for the .38 are in the can on the bottom, unfortunately."

"Got it," Joel replied and climbed over the passenger seat and into the back with Gunner. "Move over, dog."

Gunner looked disappointed that Allie wasn't joining him and stopped panting as if he realized all of the sudden that they weren't going anywhere fun.

"Aww, I'll come back there with you later." Allie reached back and scratched Gunner around his ears, then twisted around to get settled.

Ben started the truck as soon as she was faced the right way. They were already turned around and headed down the dirt road by the time she put her seatbelt on and got situated.

It only took a few minutes to backtrack to the paved road, and before long, they were on Route 40 headed east. They only made it a couple minutes before they came across the first wreck and had to slow down to maneuver around it.

Allie still hadn't gotten used to seeing them, and they really creeped her out. She tried not to pay attention to the details as they passed, which hadn't been too hard from the back seat, but not so much now.

She preferred sitting in the back with Gunner to riding up front. From the passenger seat, there was no way to avoid seeing the wrecks and the bodies trapped inside. They were right there in front of her, and the Blazer's headlights only seemed to highlight each gruesome tragedy they encountered.

At least in the back she could distract herself with Gunner or could focus on the things Ben or Joel were doing. From the back seat, she felt a little further removed from the dismal reality that existed outside the truck. Not like this, though. Now she had a front-row seat to the worst show on Earth.

· 17 ·

Only an hour into the drive and already Ben was tired of the constant swerving and breaking he had to do in order to maintain forward progress. He really had high hopes for I-70 being in better shape. They hadn't been able to get the truck over 40 miles per hour since they started, and it was frustrating.

It seemed just when they hit a section of road that was relatively free of obstacles, it was short-lived, and they had to slow down again. He was beginning to question the merit in leaving so early in the morning while it was still dark out. The old Chevy's headlights weren't the brightest, and even with the high beams on, the wrecks seemed to come up out of nowhere.

Ben thought about Jon and his family driving through the night. That must have been nerve-racking, dodging smashups all night long. It would be easy to make a mistake and clip one of these piles. Add being tired to the equation, and it was recipe for disaster.

They were lucky to have only bent a tie rod. Ben slowed a little as he thought about it. He didn't want to become one of the burnt and twisted piles of steel they were trying to avoid.

At least they were getting close to I-70, according to the road signs. It was beginning to feel like they would never get off this stretch of road. They still had over half a tank of gas left and probably another half hour or so until sunrise.

Today he would definitely let Joel share in some of the driving responsibilities. What he wouldn't give for a little more coffee right now, though. If this had been a week ago, he could have pulled into any convenience store along the way and gotten a refill, but this wasn't a week ago, and stopping somewhere now could get them killed.

It was moments like this, when the simple things they had once taken for granted only served as reminders of their old lives.

He needed to think about something else.

"How are you making out back there?" Ben glanced in the rearview mirror, but all he could see was the faint glow of Joel's red headlamp as he rummaged through the gear in the back.

"Pretty good. I found everything but the box of .38 ammo." Joel's voice was muffled as he was halfway under the blankets that covered the back of the truck.

"It should be in the box with the 9-mm ammo."

"I'll find it." Joel remained under the blanket for a few more minutes before he pulled himself out and sat back in his seat.

"Got it." Joel switched his headlamp off.

Suddenly, Ben noticed it was beginning to get a little lighter out. He looked out his window as the landscape began to brighten and show signs of the distant rising sun. It was hard to tell sometimes with the back windows mostly blacked out.

Gunner had fallen asleep long ago, having given up on the possibilities of this turning into a hunting trip, and Ben could hear him snoring on the seat behind him.

Joel pulled the small silver revolver out of its black canvas holster.

"It's unloaded." He handed the gun to Allie with the rubber grip facing her.

She took the gun from him and looked it over.

"It's smaller than I thought it would be, but it's still pretty heavy." She weighed the gun in her hand with an up-and-down motion.

"It holds six bullets and it's really easy to load." Joel reached up and showed her on the gun how to open the cylinder and where the bullets went in. Joel continued to go over the intricacies of the gun with Allie for several minutes.

Ben cracked the window a little to let some fresh air in and help wake him up a little. It was already getting stuffy in the truck, and Gunner's heavy breathing wasn't helping.

A sign up ahead reflected the light from the rising sun. The sign listed the mileage for a few upcoming towns and the exit for I-70.

"Four miles to I-70," Ben exclaimed. "We can start looking for a place to stop soon, I guess."

He counted the mile markers as they passed until he could see the exit up ahead. The sun was peeking up over the eastern horizon now and beginning to cause an uncomfortable glare through the windshield. He squinted as he steered the Blazer onto the exit ramp and gladly left Route 40 behind.

Under normal circumstances they would stay on I-70 for the majority of the trip. But they wanted to avoid some of the places on the way, so it wouldn't be that simple, unfortunately.

They would have a lot of navigating to do at some keys spots along the way. Ben wanted to take advantage of the big four-lane interstate and its wide grassy median whenever they could, though. They would use the interstate as much as possible, as long as they avoided taking any unnecessary risks.

He'd noticed on the map that I-70 seemed to skirt the outer edges of most of the towns and cities on the map and only went directly through a few. They would have to evaluate things as they went, but it was nice to see the speedometer above 50 miles per hour for a change.

There was still the occasional car or truck to avoid, but they were spaced out more, and in the wide-open landscape, he could see them coming a mile away and alter course without slowing down. The only time they slowed down significantly was if they had to cross over the grassy center median to the other side of the highway.

They only had to do this twice so far around a couple spots where bad multiple-vehicle accidents blocked the entire eastbound lane. For the most part, it was easy going and they were making good time.

The only downside was the amount of fuel they were burning. Ben swore he could actually see the needle moving toward the big orange E on the fuel gauge. He wasn't surprised. With the load they were carrying and the rooftop cargo box, they weren't exactly streamlined.

They were giving the old Blazer a workout for sure, and there wasn't a minute that went by that he didn't think about the possibilities a mechanical breakdown. He focused on all the work he and Joel had done to the truck and reassured himself they had replaced pretty much near everything that was questionable when they'd bought the vehicle.

He had made Joel a deal that when he turned 16, Ben would match whatever funds Joel had saved up to buy a car. Joel had saved over 7,000 dollars by the time he was ready to buy his truck, but what Ben hadn't counted on was his contribution coming in the form of parts and labor.

They probably had around 100 hours of labor in this truck. Nights and weekends for a couple months were spent in the garage with the Blazer on jack stands most of the time. He wouldn't have had it any other way, though, and it turned out to be a good excuse to spend lots of time with his son.

He was grateful for those memories but sad that those days were long behind them now.

· 18 ·

As Ben reminisced about the times he and Joel spent fixing up the truck, he almost didn't see the small, isolated gas station a few hundred yards off the road. It sat a little ways back off the highway, but it was a standalone building that looked empty and low risk. They would still be able to keep an eye on I-70 from there and watch for any traffic that might approach from either direction.

Ben slowed the truck and took the exit.

"Are we stopping here?" Allie asked.

"Yeah, we're really going through fuel quick. I was hoping to go a little farther, but there's no need to push it." Ben surveyed the surrounding area as he made his way to the gas station entrance.

"Looks like a good spot." Allie watched out her window as they pulled in near the gas pumps and slowly rolled past the front of the store.

Joel leaned up from the back seat to get a better look at the place.

"Looks empty, just like all the others. I can't believe every single place we've seen has been completely cleaned out like this." Joel sighed as he looked at the battered storefront.

Most of the windows were smashed, and the double glass doors at the entrance were no longer attached to the building and now lay in the parking lot several feet away, ripped off their hinges.

Joel pointed. "Somebody must have pulled those doors off with a truck or something."

"Probably." Ben continued to drive around the place until he was satisfied they were alone, finally bringing the truck to a stop by the fill caps near where they had first entered.

"Well, you know the drill." Ben shut the truck off and got out. Allie and Gunner followed with Joel not far behind. He remembered to grab the AR-15 on the way out and headed for the front of the truck while Ben got things ready to pump gas.

"When we're done filling up, we'll practice with the guns, okay?" Ben called out from the back of the truck.

"Okay. I'm ready," Allie replied.

Ben heard Joel and Allie talking as he started cranking the handle on the pump. He would let them talk while he topped off the gas tank. Joel had done it the last couple times. Besides, he was going to let Joel drive for a little while the conditions were good.

Just then, Ben heard a low rumble that sounded like it was coming toward them. He stopped turning the handle and listened, instantly on alert.

"Do you hear that?" Ben asked.

"Yeah. Sounds like it's coming from that direction." Joel pointed east down I-70.

Ben thought for a second about pulling the hose and packing up, but he thought it would be better to stand their ground against whoever was coming. If they tried to run, they wouldn't get far with the amount of gas they had in the tank anyway.

Ben left the pump hanging by the short end of the hose that ran down into the truck's fuel tank. Then he made his way over to the driver's side door. Climbing halfway in, he reached under the back seat and pulled out the padded rifle case that held his M24. He laid the case across the hood and unzipped the end just far enough to slide the rifle out.

Joel was already looking down the sights of the AR and had the magnifier flipped up. The kid learned fast.

He played with the focus on the scope. "I can see something coming around the curve way down the road, but I can't figure out what it is. I think the heat coming off the road is playing tricks on my eyes."

Ben held the Remington up and looked through his more powerful scope to get a fix on what was headed their way. Whatever it was, there was more than one. Ben started to make out a line of vehicles as they emerged from the curve in the road.

"Put your gun down, Joel. It's an Army National Guard convoy." Ben lowered his rifle and slid it back in the case.

"Really? Well, that's good, right?" Joel asked.

"Yeah, at least we know the government is still functioning on some level." Suddenly, Ben had an idea and hurried over to the truck again to grab one of the handheld radios.

He walked back to where Joel and Allie were watching the approaching convoy and turned the radio on. Pressing the scan button, he held it out in front of him and watched as it ran through the channels.

The radio paused several times as it made its way through the numbers, but he could only static until it came back around to channel six and stopped. There was no sound at first, and Ben thought maybe there was something wrong with the radio—until he heard it.

"*X-ray, X-ray come in. This is CC. Over.*"

"*CC, this is X-ray. Send it. Over.*"

"*X-ray, be advised, we are to continue on to Denver without delay. Do not offload M9s at previous destination. I repeat, do not offload M9s at previous destination. How copy? Over.*"

"*Roger Tango. Lima Charlie. X-ray is out. Over.*"

The radios sat silent on the hood of the truck once more. The conversation was brief, but at least Ben knew where they were going, although it really didn't help him and the kids much. He would rather have known where the Guard was coming from and what the conditions were like there.

"What was that all about?" Allie asked.

"Slight change of plans for them, I guess. Sounds like they're headed to Denver with those M9s. Those are the big armored bulldozers on the flat trucks. They're actually called Armored Combat Earthmovers." Ben watched as the convoy passed.

He noticed the normal lineup of ASVs (Armored Security Vehicles) and JLTVs (Joint Light Tactical Vehicles) with the occasional Humvee now and then. But what really stood out were the white buses that seemed to be traveling in threes. They were completely white and had no markings whatsoever.

"What are the buses for? I've seen National Guard convoys before, near Durango, but that's a lot of buses," Joel exclaimed.

"FEMA is my guess. Must be headed to Denver to provide relief, maybe set up a FEMA camp." Ben left the radio on the hood and put his rifle back in the truck. He returned to the hand pump and continued where he had left off with the refueling process as he kept one eye on the steady progression of vehicles passing by on the highway.

He was glad that the gas station was set back off the road now. Not that he was worried, but he was content to remain unnoticed. There wasn't anything they needed from the convoy and he didn't want to be forced into some FEMA camp for their own good.

FEMA had good intentions, but he and the kids would be better off on their own. FEMA was underfunded and notoriously incompetent in his experience. He wasn't overly concerned, though, and doubted the convoy would even stop to bother with them if they were spotted.

They were clearly in a hurry to get to Denver, where Ben guessed they would run out of supplies quickly.

· 19 ·

"Thirty-two trucks," Allie stated as they watched the last Humvee roll past and follow the long line of green and white vehicles weaving down the road.

Nothing more had come across the radio since the first transmission, which meant that they were practicing radio discipline and trying to minimize their transmissions. Ben wasn't sure why a rescue effort would do that, but he was certain there was more to that story.

"That was a good sign, right? The government is trying to help people?" Allie asked.

"Yeah, but if they're headed for Denver, it's going to take a whole lot more than the supplies they could have been carrying." Joel shook his head and looked at his dad.

"It's better than nothing, I guess, but it's going to give a lot of people a false sense of hope. And when they run out of supplies, well, it will be like

118

what Jon told us happened in Kansas City." Ben cycled the pump backward for a minute and then started to gather up the hose and stow everything.

"Do you think they're setting up emergency services in all the big cities?" Allie asked.

"I don't know. I imagine they're spread pretty thin right now." Ben noticed that Allie looked disappointed at his answer, and he was sure she was thinking about her dad in Pittsburgh.

Ben glanced back at the ever-shrinking column of vehicles and decided now was as good a time as ever.

"Allie, if you're up to it, now would be a good time to go over the shotgun and the .38. What do you think?" Ben asked.

"Sure. I'm ready." Allie straightened her posture.

Ben gathered the shotgun and the .38 pistol from the truck, along with a several rounds of ammo for each, and brought it all up to the front of the truck. He laid it all out on the hood and began to go over the shotgun with her first.

"I know Joel went over a lot of this with you already, so I'll try to stick to the basics, and if you have any questions just ask, okay?" Ben held the modified shotgun in front of him.

"Okay." Allie nodded.

"This is a semiautomatic, so that means the only time you have to set the gun up to fire is for the first shot. After that, it automatically loads another shell into the chamber and cocks the firing mechanism, making it ready to shoot again right away. It holds five shells, and you can shoot them as fast as you can pull the trigger, although it's best to take your time and conserve your shots. Always treat the gun like it's loaded, and always know where it's pointed." Ben slid three shells into the bottom of the gun.

"So far so good." Allie eyed the gun.

"It used to be a little bigger than that," Joel huffed.

Ben addressed his son's comment. "Yes, it did. And since I reduced the barrel length and turned the stock into a pistol grip, this is meant to be shot from the hip now." Ben held the gun down low and showed Allie what he meant before handing it over to her.

Allie took the gun and mimicked Ben's actions.

"Most important thing is to be comfortable and grip it firmly, but don't squeeze it too hard." Ben pointed to the bolt on the side. "Pull this lever back."

Allie pulled it back and the shell slid up into the chamber.

"Go ahead. Let it go. That's it." Ben nodded.

She released the slide lever and the action slammed the chamber shut.

CLICK.

"Okay," Ben said. "Last thing. This is the safety." He tapped it to show her. "Red means danger, and you're ready to fire."

She nodded very seriously. That attitude pleased him.

He flicked off the safety with his finger, revealing a small red dot. "Go ahead and take a few shots at that sign over there."

Allie turned to her left and squared off with a small metal sign that read ENTRANCE ONLY. She glanced back at Ben and then Joel.

"Go ahead," Joel encouraged her.

She turned around, and without any more hesitation, she pulled the trigger.

BOOM. The steel bird shot tore into the ground and lower portion of the sign post.

Allie grinned. "That wasn't as bad as I thought it was going to be."

"Aim a little higher this time." Ben nodded.

She got back into her stance and raised the gun a little.

BOOM. This time the steel shot found its mark in the center of the sign and shredded the thin metal like it was paper.

"Wow! Again?" Allie looked at Ben.

He nodded.

BOOM. Once again, the steel shot tore through the sign with ease, leaving small holes scattered across the surface.

Ben smiled. "Good job! Well done!" She was doing surprisingly well.

Joel held the AR under his arm and clapped. "Nice."

"Okay, let's see how you do with this one." Ben took the .38 off the hood and flipped the cylinder open. While Allie watched, he placed six bullets in the gun, spinning the cylinder as he loaded it.

"So this is pretty much the exact opposite as the shotgun. It's a single action revolver, which means it won't fire unless this hammer gets cocked. You can either do it manually with your thumb, or you can do it by pulling the trigger." Ben pulled the hammer down with his thumb and then let it back down slowly.

"All right," Allie said.

"You're also going to need to aim this one, so we need to find out what which eye is dominant. Hold your arm out like this." Ben held his arm out full length and stuck his thumb up.

"Now pick an object and cover it with your thumb. Let's use the sign we're shooting at."

"Okay." Allie set the shotgun down on the hood and copied Ben, holding her arm out in front of her with her thumb extended upward like she was trying to hitch a ride.

"Are you right-handed?" Ben asked.

"Yes." Allie nodded.

"Cover the sign with your thumb and close one eye. Try looking with your right eye first. Open and close your left eye, and if the sign remains behind your thumb, then that's your dominant eye."

Allie opened and closed her left eye a few times as she lined the sign up behind her thumb with her right eye. Then she switched and tried the same thing with the left eye open and closing the right one this time.

"Oh, I see what you mean. When I use my left eye to aim, the sign seems to move when I close my right eye, but the sign stays behind my thumb when I use my right eye and close the left one."

"Okay, so we know that your right eye dominant, and that's how you should aim down the pistol sights."

"Got it." Allie took the .38 from Ben as he handed it to her.

"There is no safety on that, pretty much just the hammer. It won't shoot with that hammer down." Ben thought maybe he was over explaining things, but he wanted to be sure she knew how both of these guns worked. Her life, as well as theirs, might depend on it.

Joel set the AR down on the hood of the truck for a minute and walked over to Allie, then showed her how to hold the pistol and aim down the sights properly. Then he stepped away, giving her room to shoot. "Don't worry. This one hardly kicks at all."

"Go ahead. Give it a try." Ben had considered getting ear protection out for her but decided against it.

He wanted her to be familiar with the guns, and that included the noise they made. If she needed to use either of these weapons, there wouldn't be time to put in earplugs and he didn't want her to be startled by the noise.

Ben picked up an old flattened paper cup off the ground and opened it up again as best he could. He walked over and placed it on top of the sign post.

"Try and shoot the cup. Take as many shots as you want." Ben jogged back to a safe spot behind her and waited, arms crossed.

Allie lined up the sights and aimed at the crumpled paper cup.

Bang… Bang. On the second shot, the cup fell to the ground.

"Nice!" Joel nodded.

"I think you're a natural." Ben smiled. "Go ahead and shoot the rest at the sign if you want."

Allie turned her attention back to the sign without hesitation and fired the gun. *Bang… Bang… Bang… Bang.*

Ben could see where at least three of the four shots hit the sign and made larger holes than the smaller buckshot.

"That's really good." He was genuinely impressed with Allie's shooting skills and thought maybe she was more prepared to take on this harsh new world than he realized.

"For your first time, that's awesome! Believe me, we've seen a lot worse at the range, right, Dad?" Joel looked at Ben.

"That's for sure." Ben shook his head as he began to gather things up off the hood. He handed Allie the box of bullets and small holster that went with the .38.

"It's your gun now. I would like you to keep it with you any time you're outside the truck." Ben looked at Allie. "And keep it loaded because it's just a paperweight without those." He motioned at the box of bullets.

She cradled the weapon in her hands. "Thank you. I'll take good care of it."

"I'll show you how to unload and load it if you want," Joel offered.

"I can do it. It's my gun after all." Allie smiled.

"Come on, Gunner. Let's go." Ben called out to the dog, who was sniffing around a dumpster in the other corner of the parking lot when he heard his name.

He looked up to see them loading the truck and paused for a moment before he realized they were leaving. Racing across the parking lot, he leapt into the Blazer without breaking his stride, nearly knocking Joel over.

"Whoa there, dog! Take it easy," Joel scolded.

"How do you feel about driving for a while?" Ben asked.

"Sure." Joel headed around to the driver's side.

Gunner was already getting situated in the back with Allie. She was working out how to attach the holster to her belt as Ben climbed into the passenger seat and slid the shotgun back under the rear seat.

He watched her for a second. "There's no right or wrong way really, just whatever feels comfortable and makes the gun easy for you to grab quickly with your strong hand. Joel and I each wear ours differently. Plus, he's left-hand dominant. So just do whatever feels right for you."

"Thanks, I will." Allie played with the position of the holster on her belt for a little bit while Joel started the truck up and pulled out onto the access road that led to I-70.

· 20 ·

Allie glanced out the window from time to time. Ben hadn't been kidding when he said there wasn't much to look at in Kansas.

The scenery was the same, regardless of how much time had passed since she last looked. She could see how the landscape might be enjoyable on a normal road trip, with the vast openness of it all, but now it only served as a reminder of the distance they had yet to travel to get to her dad.

Would they see more National Guard troops along the way? Maybe her dad would be all right in Pittsburgh if help was showing up. Surely there would be a FEMA camp or other type of support effort in the larger cities.

Still, she knew Pittsburgh had some bad sections not too far from her dad's place. She had passed them on the school bus every day when she lived there.

Between the convoy sighting and being newly entrusted with the responsibility of the .38 pistol, she felt surprisingly optimistic for a change.

Her initial doubts about Ben wanting to have her come along had all but evaporated now. He trusted her enough to give her a gun, and she was determined not to let him or Joel down. Her feeling of guilt about being an extra burden on Joel and Ben was slowly being replaced with a sense of responsibility and belonging.

She still felt bad about Ben and Joel having to rescue her, even though they both assured her it was nothing to worry about. Just the thought of the whole ordeal gave her the chills, and she tried to push the dirty faces of her captors out of her mind.

She vowed then and there to do her best not to let her guard down again. She was determined to be a help to Joel and his dad and not a hindrance. She wondered how much farther along on their journey to Joel's brother and sister they would be if it wasn't for her and her insistence on using the restrooms at their fuel stops. She couldn't do that to them anymore. She'd have to forgo the luxury of a proper bathroom and make due otherwise from here on out. Besides, the conditions were getting less and less tolerable.

The last couple bathrooms she had used were beyond disgusting.

She glanced at Ben. Being responsible for her and Joel while trying to get to his other children must have weighed heavily on him. Not knowing if his other two kids were okay or not had to be a constant thought.

At that moment, Allie realized how much of a sacrifice it was for Ben and Joel to get her to Pittsburgh, knowing that they must feel the same way she did about the odds of actually finding her dad.

Ben and Joel were doing their best to put a positive spin on it, but she knew the chances weren't good, and there was a feeling of futility to the effort that she was certain they felt as well.

What would she do if they found her dad? Would she stay in Pittsburgh with him? How could he take care of her? She might have to take care of him by the time they got there.

She stared out at the blank landscape. For the first time she was beginning to have thoughts about the possibility of her and her dad continuing on with Ben and Joel. Allie didn't want to think about the fact that she might never see Joel or Ben or Gunner again if she stayed in Pittsburgh.

Allie looked down at Gunner, who was breathing heavily as he drifted off to sleep. His large head weighed heavily on her leg as she rubbed the soft fur on his ear. She'd come to love this silly dog. Her eyes began to water as she thought about life without them.

How could she ask them to take on the added responsibility, though? They had already done so much for her. The last thing she wanted to do was burden them even more with her father.

He was good with computers, but he would be lost without modern conveniences. Who was she kidding? He would probably starve if it weren't for the Chinese takeout place around the block from his apartment.

He would be more of a liability than an asset.

Allie loved her father dearly, and they had a decent relationship, albeit a long-distance one. They FaceTimed and emailed each other often and never went more than a few days without at least texting.

Moving with her mother was one of the hardest choices she ever had to make, and it had broken her heart a little to leave her father behind. But he worked long hours and often weekends as well. At least her mother had a few days off in a row between shifts and was around more.

There were many times when her dad had missed her field hockey games because of work responsibilities. He had bought into the software company where he had worked a couple years ago, and since then, she felt like he was more concerned about the company's welfare than hers and her mom's.

The two other partners at the company were

younger and single. Allie had heard her mother argue with her dad on more than one occasion about how they were asking too much of her father at work and didn't understand what it meant to have family priorities.

With the opening of a second location in Raleigh, North Carolina, Allie's dad had begun to travel on top of his already busy schedule. That was the last straw for Allie's mom, who'd realized things weren't getting any better for their marriage.

She'd decided to call it quits. Her mom had never been fond of Pittsburgh anyway. She'd taken the opportunity to accept a job in Durango in an effort to improve their quality of life. At least that was what she told Allie. And for the most part, it *had* improved their lives.

Adjusting to the change had been hard at first, but the people she met in Durango seemed nice, and she made friends quickly because of field hockey. She had never really been fond of Pittsburgh, either, so it wasn't hard to embrace the clean air and the beautiful landscape Durango had to offer.

Getting to spend a few days a week with her mom had been good, too. They had just gotten into hiking a few months ago and hadn't even scratched the surface on the trails around Durango. Allie and her mom were looking forward to exploring some new areas on her days off this summer. Allie had picked out a few trails that promised wonderful views and breathtaking waterfalls.

But none of that would ever happen now.

· 21 ·

They gave Topeka and Kansas City a generous berth as they skirted the edge of both cities. Ben thought he probably went a little farther around each one than he needed to, but he wasn't taking any chances. Based on the information he had, he knew both places were trouble, so there was no need to feel bad about the extra time it took to navigate around the cities. Being cautious was well worth the extra effort and navigation.

Besides, a more direct route could have cost them a lot more than time.

They were able to make good time otherwise on I-70, when they did use it, and Ben found himself able to actually exceed the speed limit for long distances. Slowing down to avoid hazards had become the exception, rather than the rule, on the big multi-lane road.

This is what he'd hoped to find, figuring that traffic would have been light on this road at the time of the EMP attacks and mostly limited to trucks and the occasional car.

His assumption proved to be true for the most part, and the large remains of the 18-wheelers were easy to spot from a distance and avoid without slowing down at all.

Of course, they paid for the speed with frequent stops for fuel, but they could time it with their deviations from the interstate and take advantage of the safety the secondary roads.

They also benefited from the opportunities the lesser roads provided in the way of smaller gas stations to top off the tanks on the thirsty Blazer.

Ben felt better at these smaller, out-of-the-way locations. Less population usually meant less chance of trouble. But he knew the landscape would change soon and they would be forced to refuel in some less desirable areas in the not too distant future.

The mood in the truck improved briefly when they passed the sign that welcomed them to Missouri. Small talk filled the cab for a while as they speculated on things to come.

But the feeling of progress diminished as the unrelenting road, seemingly unchanged despite all their hard hours of driving, stretched out in front of them.

When they passed the sign saying they still had 87 miles to go before the first exit to St. Louis, Ben began to realize that his hope of getting through a good portion of Illinois was probably a little too ambitious for the day.

It was already well into the afternoon, and if he stuck to the travel plan they would most likely end up at the Illinois border around six, maybe a little earlier depending on the roads after he got off the interstate.

He planned on going around St. Louis to the north and stopping at the Mississippi River to take a break before they continued on, but by the looks of things, they would make camp along the river instead tonight. That would be a good place to stop. They would have plenty of fresh water and with any luck could catch some dinner.

He was grateful for the dehydrated food, but a change of menu would be welcome. There were only so many times he could look forward to eating: beans and rice or some kind of pasta with a protein substitute other than meat. The fact that he and Joel had been eating like that on the camping trip the day before it all happened didn't help any, either.

"I think the best we can hope for today is to make it to the Mississippi River," Ben announced.

"How much farther is that?" Allie asked.

"I think we could be close in another couple hours, with a fuel stop in there as well," Ben answered. They had a little better than three-quarters of a tank and had about another hour or so of driving before he would get off the main road and start to wind around St. Louis. They had enough gas to get to a campsite, but he wanted to make sure they had as close to a full tank of gas as possible for the next morning.

"I wonder what kind of fish are in the Mississippi," Joel said.

"Bass, catfish, bluegills, and crappie," Ben said. "And probably lots more I don't know about. It's really big water."

"I hope I can catch something we can eat." Joel grinned as he looked back at Allie.

But Ben had more pressing concerns on his mind. There were limited ways across the Mississippi, and they would all be through highly populated areas. The bridges would be choke points that could easily be jammed by an accident or, even worse, a roadblock.

If the bridge was impassable, they would have no choice but to drive to another crossing point and hope for the best. Unfortunately, the river crossings were few and far apart. This could put them behind schedule by a day or more if they chose poorly.

Ben had been looking at one spot in particular on the map. Alton was the name of the town, and it was on the Illinois side of the river. He'd never been to the place or even heard of it, but it looked like a smallish town.

His map showed a waterfowl sanctuary on the otherwise uninhabited western bank of the river. That could be the perfect place to camp tonight. The sanctuary was highlighted in green on his map and was located between the Missouri River and the Mississippi River on a small peninsula that ended where the two merged together.

They would have to cross two bridges, which he wasn't thrilled about, but it looked like the least populated route. Alton was on the other side of the Mississippi River, and they could pass through quickly in the early morning hours without any trouble if they were lucky.

The next nearest crossing was to their south, but it came close to passing through the center of St. Louis. He thought that was too risky. Going that way would certainly lead to trouble. To the north was another bridge, but it would take a few hours to get there and a few hours back to I-70. He knew that would realistically take them a day out of their way, and that was farther from I-70 than he wanted to go.

Joel had the atlas open on his lap. "So where were you thinking tonight then?"

"See that green area there?" Ben glanced over and pointed to the spot.

"Hey, it's a waterfowl sanctuary. Maybe we could bag a few ducks? It's not like there's anyone enforcing the season." Joel raised his brows.

"Yeah, I thought about that, but fishing is quieter. We'll have to see what it looks like when we get to the campsite. It would be a nice change to have a little duck for dinner." Ben grinned.

Joel seemed excited at the prospect, and Ben knew Gunner would be more than happy to help. Just this little bit of talk about hunting had been enough to rouse the dog from his nap.

His big brown head came up.

"You're too smart for your own good, boy. He must have heard the magic word." Joel reached back to give Gunner a few scratches on his head.

"And what word is that?" Allie asked.

"Duck." Joel looked at Gunner when he said it, causing the dog to tilt his head to the side.

"Don't go getting him worked up. We still have another hour or so of being cooped up in here," Ben warned.

The sign ahead had the exit mileage for Route 67. About 15 more miles and they would get off the interstate and head north for another half hour or so, by his estimation.

With each passing mile, their surroundings transformed. For the last hour or so, the density of houses and buildings had steadily increased. More houses and more buildings meant more people— and more possibility for trouble.

Was he being reckless bringing them this way? He had debated this section of the route in his mind before reluctantly settling on coming this way. It was closer than he wanted to be to an area with this size of a population, but the other options would cost them days in time.

And those days might mean the difference in seeing his kids again or not.

· 22 ·

Ben was happy to keep up the pace they were setting by using the interstate, but it came at a cost. He felt like a moving target as they sped through the increasingly congested areas. They had passed a few random people along the sides of the road and seen more down the side streets.

The people they saw seemed to be lost in their own little world, and only a few looked up to watch them go by. At least maintaining a decent rate of speed through here meant there was no chance for any interaction.

There was no doubt in Ben's mind that most people's supplies had run out by now, if not earlier. By now, all the stores had been cleaned out and looted and there would be no point in scavenging for supplies at those types of places anymore.

He thought that might actually be good for them and translate to empty gas stations when they stopped along the way. Most people would stay indoors if they still had a house or a place to hide.

But some people might not have either of those.

Some areas they had been through had entire blocks burned to the ground. Row after row of streets lined with charred remains of what were once neighborhoods. Some of the larger debris piles still gave off small trails of smoke that wafted into the already thick air, leaving an acrid tang that stuck in the back of his throat.

They had definitely seen a decline in the air quality as they'd gotten closer to St. Louis. Looking to the southeast toward the city, they could now see what was causing it. A thick, dark cloud of smoke seemed to cover the entire sky over the city. A smaller column of blackish gray smoke rose up several miles into the atmosphere and pushed up into the larger cloud at the center.

Joel leaned toward the window. "St. Louis must be completely destroyed."

"Wow," Allie whispered.

"Yeah, that looks pretty bad. Maybe…" Ben paused.

"What?" Joel turned to look at him.

Ben quickly rethought his plan. "Maybe we stay on the interstate and get through here as fast as possible. We can always camp on the other side near the river. If we stay on 70 for another 15 minutes past the exit, we'll be at the bridge just outside of the city. It's far enough away from that."

He nodded in the direction of the looming smoke cloud. "I didn't expect the road to be this open this close to the city. Maybe there aren't that many people left around here. Staying on 70 would save us a lot of time compared to going north to Alton."

He rubbed his ever-thickening beard. This was the longest he'd gone without shaving in a while. And he noticed more gray than he remembered when he looked in the rearview mirror.

"Sounds good to me." Allie nodded her approval from the back seat.

"I guess it wouldn't hurt to check it out." Joel slumped down in his seat a little.

"What's wrong?" Ben asked.

Joel shrugged. "I was hoping to get a few ducks for us."

"You will have plenty of opportunities for that in the days ahead. We're getting ready to drive through some of the best waterfowl areas in the country." Ben shook his head. The kid loved his hunting.

"Okay." Joel sighed as he sat up a little.

Ben reached over and shook Joel's shoulder. "We'll take a look as long as the road stays like this."

They could use a break. It had been a long day of driving and they were all tired—at least Ben knew he was. It wasn't like him to change plans spur of the moment, but when an opportunity presented itself, he couldn't pass it up.

The road was in good shape and the obstacles were still spaced far enough apart to make travel easy. They were able to maintain speeds above 40 miles per hour pretty consistently. Plus, they had plenty of gas to make it over the bridge and into Illinois if the bridge was clear. If it wasn't, they would only have to backtrack a few miles to pick up an alternate route that would take them toward Alton. It would be foolish not to at least check the shortest route across the river.

By the enormity of the cloud that hung over the city, Ben imagined there was nothing left of St. Louis. The place was probably a wasteland by now, which meant there shouldn't be too many people around.

If the city was destroyed, people would try to get away from there. With any luck, they could get across the bridge and do the same.

· 23 ·

Joel knew his dad had been right. The interstate remained open enough for them to continue toward the bridge. Eventually, the mixed residential and business buildings gave way to a more light industrial area with more open space.

The air was heavy now with a strong burnt smell that reminded Joel of a plastic bag he had once accidentally dropped into a campfire. The smoke from the city, aided by a warm breeze, drifted in their direction. It settled over the road like a thick fog.

Joel noticed his dad had slowed down quite a bit now from how fast they had been going just a few minutes ago.

"It's getting pretty thick." Joel squinted as the smoke stung his nostrils and eyes a little. Even the sun couldn't get through.

"I'd turn around if it was any farther, but the bridge is just up ahead. We should see it any minute now."

Joel glanced back at Allie and Gunner to see how they were coping with the smoke. Allie had her shirt pulled up over her mouth and nose. Gunner was sitting up straight on the seat next to her and let out a big sneeze.

"Can you guys hang in there for a few minutes more?" Ben asked.

"Yeah, just keep going," Joel answered.

Allie motioned with her hand to keep driving. "I'm okay. It just smells bad more than anything."

Ben continued on at an even slower speed than before. Joel glanced over at the speedometer and noticed they were only going about 15 miles per hour.

"There's the sign," Allie mumbled through her shirt collar.

Joel read the road sign out loud as they drove past. "Chain of Rocks Bridge."

Less than a minute later they were on the divided, four-lane bridge. There was no shoulder on the bridge, only a guardrail separating them from the drop-off to the water below. The smoke was so thick that only a few car lengths ahead were visible. They were really creeping along now.

Joel strained to see the river below but only caught fleeting glimpses through the almost opaque smoke that was getting worse somehow now that they were out on the open bridge.

Suddenly Ben slammed on the brakes, causing the Blazer to screech to a stop. Less than 10 feet in front of the truck, the bridge abruptly ended. They sat in silence for a minute, staring at the mangled and jagged concrete that was all that remained of the structure.

Ben put the Blazer in park and got out. Joel followed, with Allie right behind him.

"Don't let Gunner out," Ben called back to them.

"Sorry, boy, stay." Allie slowly closed the door behind her, trapping Gunner in the truck on the front seat, where he had moved to in anticipation of following them.

They slowly inched to within a couple feet of where the concrete ended. From that perilous point, they looked down.

Joel couldn't see more than a few feet into the abyss, and it seemed like it could have gone on forever. It was one of the weirdest things he had ever seen as he watched the thick smoke drift under them.

"I wonder what happened. I mean, bridges don't just collapse," Joel said.

Ben put his hands on his hips and shook his head as he stood at the guardrail that separated the four lanes. "I don't know, but both sides are out. I guess I was hoping for too much. We'll have to head up to Alton after all."

Joel looked at his dad but could only make out the dull shape of his figure, even though he was less than 20 feet away from where Joel was standing. The smoke was just that thick.

Just then, a breeze kicked up out of nowhere and stirred the smoke into a frenzy, briefly exposing the cause of the bridge's collapse. Joel turned to Allie and then back to the drop-off, making sure she was seeing what he was seeing. His eyes followed the bent and twisted rebar that cascaded over the edge toward the water.

Hunks of soot-covered metal were tangled up in the structure that led down to what was unmistakably the tail section of an airplane. He began to read the numbers on the tail but lost sight of everything as the wind calmed and the heavy smoke settled back over the wreckage like a blanket.

"Did you see that?" Joel asked.

"What? No." Allie strained to see over the jagged edge without daring to venture any closer. "What was it?"

"A plane, or at least part of it. That's what took the bridge out." The moment he finished speaking, he thought about how this might affect Allie. He was glad she was standing a few feet behind him and hadn't seen the wreckage. He was sure this would bring to mind her mother and the fate she had most likely suffered.

Ben headed back to the truck. "Let's get out of here."

Joel was more than happy to get away from the edge and return to the truck. He wasn't sure why, but the smoke was bothering him more all of the sudden and he felt like he could almost taste it now. He pulled his shirt over his nose and joined Allie, who was already getting settled into the back seat.

She hadn't responded to what he said about the plane, and he wondered if she was all right.

Ben sighed as he backed up and got the truck turned around. "I should have known. That would have been too easy. Should have just stuck to the plan."

Joel thought his dad must have been worried about Allie, too, as he seemed to be expediting their departure. Or maybe he just wanted to get them out the smoke.

Either way, Joel was glad to get away. The whole place had an eerie feel to it, and he couldn't wait to see the sun again.

"At least it wasn't too far out of the way." Joel glanced back at Allie, who had occupied herself with Gunner. She was leaning into him, and her hair covered her face. Joel decided to give her some time and resituated himself forward so he could help his dad navigate.

"Look at the map and see if there's a quicker way back to 67, will you?" Ben asked.

"Okay." Joel pulled out the atlas that was already open to their location and found an alternate road quickly.

"The next exit we come to will take us there." Joel followed the road with his finger on the map as he traced a line all the way to the waterfowl sanctuary between the two bridges outside Alton. "It shouldn't be too far."

The exit came up fast and Ben steered the truck north onto it.

A hospital sat on the other side of the highway, where the ramp made a long winding curve down off the interstate. The building was still intact and standing, but the first-floor windows were all shattered and it had that same empty look that all the buildings had now.

It made Joel think about how truly alone they were. There was nowhere to go if they got hurt or had an emergency. Then he thought about the bridge and the plane crash and how that would stay that way for who knew how long. Maybe forever.

No one had come to check for survivors. No one would come to clean up, and no one would come to rebuild the bridge.

It really was just them against the world now.

· 24 ·

They continued on the secondary road for a few miles in silence. That was fine with Ben; he needed to concentrate. He was already tired from driving all day, and the smoke was still making it tricky to navigate. The air was improving as they drove away from St. Louis, but it was still far from good.

Allie broke the silence. "It will be nice to get away from this smoke. It's already a little better."

Ben was glad to hear from her. He was concerned about how that scene back there had affected her. He wasn't sure how much she had seen of it. But he saw the airplane and knew it would strike a nerve with her.

He should have had both kids wait in the truck while he checked the other lanes, but it was too late now. Besides, that wouldn't be the last plane crash they'd see—he was sure of it. He was honestly surprised they hadn't seen more, especially after he and Joel had witnessed that crash on their hike back that first morning.

Joel breathed in deeply without the shirt over his nose. "It's definitely getting better."

"We ought to be at the campsite in half an hour or so. I'm not going to stop for gas. We still have well over half a tank, and I can top it off with the two spare cans on the back when we get there. We can gas up tomorrow," Ben stated. He didn't have it in him right now to go through the process of refueling, and they had plenty of gas to keep them going for a while. He was just glad to be driving away from the city.

"Sounds good to me." Joel nodded.

The mood in the truck seemed to improve along with the quality of the air. Before long, the heaviness of the smoke lifted, and they emerged into the late afternoon sun once again. It was like a whole other world existed beyond that cloud of smoke, which still hung heavily on the horizon behind them.

The small businesses and fast food places gradually turned into residential neighborhoods, and then eventually the houses thinned out into mostly open fields and trees. Ben saw the sign for the first of the two bridges they would need to cross.

Please let the bridges be clear, he thought. The next time he stopped the truck, he wanted it to be where they were going to spend the night.

Along both sides of the road they passed a huge limestone quarry operation that sat on the edge of the river. Ben imagined the place in its glory, with train cars and barges being loaded and shipped out all over the country. It would be a busy place normally.

But now it only served as a reminder of how things had come grinding to a halt, like the heavy equipment scattered around the quarry property and sitting idle and wasting away. Some of them reminded him of tombstones as they sat parked on top of the light gray hills of gravel.

As they approached the bridge, they all leaned forward in their seats, scanning the road ahead through the dusty windshield.

"Looks good from here. Couple cars here and there, but it looks like we can get around them," Joel said.

"Yeah, it doesn't look too bad," Ben added.

The Missouri River was much smaller than the Mississippi where they had tried the other bridge and was only about a quarter of a mile wide here. Ben could see all the way to the other side easily, and it looked clear to cross. He noticed several cars near the middle of the bridge that looked a little out of place considering the rest of the bridge was clear. They were too organized—almost like someone lined them up along the sides of the road. Fortunately, there was enough room down the center to squeeze by.

"Boy, the water is really brown. Is it always like that?" Joel sounded disappointed.

"I think so. It's a little different from back home, huh?" Ben replied.

The water here was nothing like the rivers in Colorado. He could tell this river was deeper and ran with purpose. The water moved swiftly as mini whirlpools swirled in and out of existence randomly across the surface. The water was a dark brown, somewhere between chocolate milk and coffee, the opposite of the clear water they were used to in the Rockies.

Ben wondered if the river was even fishable like this or if it would be a waste of time. Maybe they could find calmer waters once they were in the waterfowl sanctuary.

"I don't know about fishing here, Dad. I wouldn't even know where to start." Joel stared blankly out his window.

"You're reading my mind, but don't try to hide the fact that you're happy about not being able to fish so you can talk me into letting you try for some ducks." Ben chuckled.

"You boys," Allie joked.

Ben didn't want to say anything to diminish the mood in the truck. They could all use a little morale boost.

So he didn't say anything to the kids, but the group of cars at the center of the bridge still had his attention. They were close enough now that he could count six cars. None of them were wrecked or even looked damaged, but they were all newer-model sedans and minivans that wouldn't have been in running condition because of their computer systems.

He thought it strange, nonetheless, to have six of them like that in the middle of the bridge. He would have crossed over to the southbound lanes of the bridge and given the odd cars a wide berth, but the concrete barrier in the median prevented it. Instead, he was forced to drive between them. He put his hand a little closer to his gun.

Ben half expected someone to jump out from behind them at any moment, but nothing happened and they passed by the cars without incident.

Glad he hadn't said anything to the kids, he eased his hand away from the center console and the Desert Eagle.

The rest of the bridge, as well as the road beyond, was clear ahead, and Ben picked up speed. The same, however, could not be said for the southbound lanes on the other side.

As they neared the end of the bridge, a truck was jackknifed firmly between the guardrail and the concrete divider, completely blocking both southbound lanes. That was exactly the type of thing he had been worried about.

He was thankful now for the tall concrete divider that stopped the truck and kept their lanes open. They were across this bridge, but they still had one more to cross a few miles ahead at the Mississippi River.

· 25 ·

Ben didn't want to get too close to the second bridge tonight. He preferred to camp on the smaller river if possible.

Alton didn't look like a large town on the map, but it was located directly on the other side of the Mississippi and they would be too close to a populated area for Ben's liking if they went all the way to the next bridge before stopping.

As badly as he wanted to know if the road was clear ahead, it was time to stop. He took the next right into a heavily wooded area and followed the gravel road back toward the river. The road came to a tee, with one part of it heading back under the bridge and upstream to their right.

They went left and followed the dirt road in the opposite direction downstream. Within a few minutes, the road turned into trail barely wide enough for the Blazer to slip through. The occasional branch and bush scraped the sides of the truck as they made their way deeper into the woods and away from the road.

They followed the trail until it ended on a small section of wide riverbank that led up to a fairly level grassy area that looked like a great spot to set up camp.

"Looks good to me." Joel opened the door as soon as Ben put the truck in park and turned it off.

The river went around a bend a couple hundred yards farther down from where they were, and the elevation dropped off into a low-lying marshy area.

"That must be part of the waterfowl area," Ben noted.

Gunner forced his way out of the truck ahead of Allie and launched himself off the passenger's seat. He hit the ground running and made a wide circle around the Blazer, sniffing as he went before making a beeline for the water.

Without slowing down, he flew over the sandy bank and crashed into the river, only stopping when he was chest-deep in the muddy water. He stood there panting for a minute before he lapped at the brown water, then waded back to the small sandy beach.

"I don't think he cares what color the water is," Allie commented as she climbed down from the truck and joined Ben and Joel at the tailgate, where they were already unloading the gear.

"Well, since Gunner's already wet, you might as well try to get a few ducks before we lose too much more daylight." Ben glanced south in the direction of the marsh, then at his son. Joel's face lit up with excitement. "After you get your tent set up, okay?"

"Yep." Joel grinned and hastily gathered the remainder of his things from the rooftop cargo box.

Ben had mixed feelings about Joel shooting ducks, but they could use some protein that didn't come out of a bag for a change. There was nothing like a good meal over a campfire to lift the spirits, and they could use it. They had done well today, even though they hadn't gotten as far as he would have liked. Despite that, he still considered the day a success.

They had made good time and avoided any real trouble, and that was a win these days.

This was a pretty remote spot, too. Far enough off the road where a few rounds from the shotgun wouldn't attract any attention.

Plus, they hadn't seen a soul since they got off the interstate, so this was as good a place as any to take advantage of nature's cupboard. He had planned from the beginning to supplement their food reserves with wild game, so why not?

He also had to admit that part of the reason he wanted Joel to go was so the boy could have a little fun. God knew he deserved it. They all did. He was hoping Allie would join him. It would be a good distraction for them both while he got a fire going and relaxed for a little while.

He moved some blankets around the back of the truck and noticed the two old shotguns they had taken from Allie's abductors the other day. He had all but forgotten about the old rusty guns.

Ben pulled them out and heaved the smaller shotgun that had been shortened into the river. He took a few steps toward the water before he tossed the other larger gun in as well.

"Why'd you do that?" Joel asked.

"They were in bad shape, and neither one was safe to shoot. More likely to hurt yourself than what you're shooting at with those." Ben walked back to the truck and grabbed three 20-gauge shotgun shells out of the back and handed them to Joel. "Three is all you get. Make 'em count."

Ben was willing to let him hunt, but he didn't want him going through a box of shells while chasing ducks around the marsh. There wasn't much shooting light left anyways.

Joel grabbed his modified Weatherby out of the truck and looked at the now shortened barrel. "This should be interesting."

Ben glanced at Joel. "Better get close."

"Yeah," Joel said before glancing at Allie. "Do you want to come?" Joel bit his lip.

"Sure, as long as I won't be in the way," she answered.

"No. Come on, it'll be fun," Joel insisted as he started backpedaling toward the marsh.

Allie threw her sleeping bag into her tent and zipped it up before she hurried to catch up with Joel. Gunner was already ahead of them by 20 feet and panting with excitement.

Ben quickly lost sight of the kids as they threaded into the cattails and reeds. He heard Joel tell Gunner to heel up to keep the dog from scaring the ducks before they even got there.

He shook his head, smiling. He wasn't too confident in the prospects of having duck for dinner, but it almost didn't matter. Sure, it would be nice, but it was rewarding enough to see them have a little break from reality.

Joel would have his work cut out for him. A sawed-off shotgun without a buttstock would increase the difficulty of shooting a duck out of the sky mid-flight by quite a bit. Still, though, it was out of season and maybe they could get in close.

There were definitely ducks in there. He could hear them occasionally in the distance among the marsh grass.

After his tent was squared away for the night, Ben began digging two holes for the fire. He dug them a few inches apart, one bigger than the other. Once he had them at the size and depth he wanted, he reached down into the larger one and dug a small tunnel connecting the two holes together at the bottom.

Then he filled the bottom of the larger one with dried grass and a few twigs. Fortunately, the riverbank was littered with dead wood and branches that had washed up long ago when the water had been high. Having been beached some time ago and left to bake in the sun, most of the wood he found was dry and brittle. Perfect for burning, he thought, as he gathered it up in his arms.

Before long he had a respectable pile of various-sized sticks assembled next to the fire pit.

The dry grass at the bottom lit easily with a flick of the lighter, and he was adding larger material into the hole in no time. He topped it off with a couple pieces from a thick branch he chopped up with the hatchet.

He stepped back for a minute to catch his breath and admire his work. The two-hole system was working well and there was very little smoke escaping from the fire.

He could already feel the warmth, and even though it was pleasant out, there was just something about a fire that always seemed to put his mind at ease. He stared at the flames as they began to lick the edges of the larger pieces on top.

Just then, in the distance, he heard the shotgun twice in quick succession and then again a few seconds later. Ben was bolstered with a sudden sense of confidence and headed over to the truck to grab a pot and something to go with the duck if Joel had been successful.

He started heating up the water for the rice and beans over the fire pit before finding himself a reasonably comfortable spot to sit against an old dead tree while waiting for them to return.

It wasn't long before Gunner, still dripping wet, came running out of the tall grass. His tail was wagging as fast as he could manage, flinging water off the end in both directions. Gunner headed straight to the fire and stopped to shake himself free of the excess water.

Joel and Allie weren't far behind, and Ben could see Joel holding two mallards by their necks as they emerged from the brush. Once they were a little closer, Joel held up the birds for Ben to see.

"I got two!" Joel smiled proudly.

"Good job, bud!" Ben nodded.

"I never realized ducks flew that fast." Allie came over and stood by the fire.

Joel put the gun down on the tailgate and laid the ducks out for his dad's inspection.

"Nice work. They're a good size, too!" Ben looked the birds over. "Let's take them down to the water and get them breasted out." Ben didn't have the energy to pluck the birds clean. Most of the meat was in the breast anyway, which he could dice up easily and mix in with the rice and beans.

"Allie, while we get the ducks ready, would you keep an eye on the water and get the food started when it boils?" Ben asked.

"Sure, no problem." Allie smiled up at them from her seat by the fire. She looked more than content to stay put and enjoy the warmth.

"I got them." Joel grabbed the ducks and led the way to the river. Ben was glad they ended up here, and for the moment, he was the happiest he'd been in a long time. He felt incredibly lucky to have his son and Allie with him. And he had hope he would get to see Bradley and Emma soon. That was more than a lot of people had right now.

The duck was a good addition to the beans and rice, and everyone devoured their portion in near silence. Even Gunner got a few spoonfuls over his dry food as a reward for his retrieval of the ducks.

After dinner, the kids filled Ben in on the details of the hunt, and they sat around the fire for a little while and talked.

Ben was considering sleeping outside the tent near the fire but changed his mind when he swatted a mosquito on his arm.

"Well, guys, I'm gonna call it a night. I won't be happy with anything less than Ohio tomorrow, so unfortunately it's going to be another early morning. Don't stay up too late, Joel. I'd like you to help with the driving a little tomorrow."

"Okay, Dad. No problem."

"Oh, and would you top off the—" Ben stopped mid-sentence as Joel held up the water filter in his hand.

"Way ahead of you." Joel grinned.

"Well done. Good night." Ben went to brush his teeth over by the truck and left his empty water bottle on the tailgate for Joel. He stood there for a minute, looking up at the stars before finally crawling into his tent. Exhausted from the day, he didn't make it far and fell asleep on top of his sleeping bag.

· 26 ·

Ben immediately knew it was later than he'd wanted to wake up. He could see a faint light through the thin tent material coming from the east, and birds were chirping in the nearby trees.

He rubbed his eyes and glanced at his watch. Almost six in the morning. He was hoping to be on the road by then.

He forced himself to sit up and unzip the tent flap. The fire was still going, although it was reduced to just embers at the bottom. Ben could see the heat rising as it distorted the air over the hole. That would make coffee a little easier to get started.

He looked over at Joel's and Allie's tents and saw no movement from either of them.

"Hey guys? It's time to get up," Ben called out as he pulled himself from his tent and set about making coffee.

The kids had left the water bottles neatly lined up across the rear bumper. Ben grabbed one of the bottles and washed down a few pills for his shoulder. The joints had a tendency to bother him a little on long road trips. Sleeping on the ground like this didn't help, either.

Looking half asleep, Joel and Allie slowly emerged from their tents. Not much was said other than a couple halfhearted good mornings as everyone went about the routine of breaking down tents and rolling bags.

Not until after they all had a cup of coffee in their hands did they come to life and discuss the plan for the day.

Allie took advantage of the fire Ben had rekindled for the coffee and made them all apple cinnamon oatmeal with a little honey drizzled on top that she had brought from the house. They took a quick break from packing up camp and sat down to eat as they talked.

The hot food and coffee gave Ben the jolt he needed, and he decided to drive first. He was considering having Joel take the first shift but maybe after they got into Illinois and back onto I-70.

If the interstate was anything like what they had seen yesterday, maybe he could even get a couple hours of sleep in the back and Allie could sit up front with Joel and navigate.

But Ben was getting ahead of himself. They had to get across that bridge first. He thought about the

18-wheeler they'd seen wedged across the bridge yesterday, and then he remembered those oddly placed cars they'd passed in the middle. He had forgotten about how much they'd bothered him yesterday, and the more he thought about it, the more it began to worry him again.

"You guys ready to hit the road?" Ben suddenly felt a renewed sense of urgency to get out of there and get moving. He got to work cleaning up and used his foot to push the dirt he'd dug out last night back into the fire pit, snuffing it out quickly.

"Yep. I'm ready," Allie chirped.

"Yeah, I'm good. Want me to drive?" Joel offered.

"Later. For sure. You can drive next time we stop for gas." Ben patted Joel on the back before he headed for the driver's side of the truck. They all got in and assumed their usual spots for the ride.

They slowly made their way back out through the small trail they'd driven in on. Their heads bobbed back and forth as the Blazer rolled along the washed-out ruts, scraping a few branches as they went. Finally, the trail opened up to dirt road that felt smooth compared to what they had just driven over.

"That's better," Allie said from the back seat, where Gunner was using her to maintain his balance.

They followed the dirt road back toward the bridge and made the turn to get back on the paved road when Ben slammed on the breaks hard enough to cause Gunner to slide off the bench and land on the floor at Allie's feet.

"What the—!" Joel braced himself on the dashboard.

Ben quickly put the truck in reverse and maneuvered it down alongside the bridge, all the way to the tee in the road. He swung the end of the truck around at the intersection and threw it into drive, getting them back down the road they had just come out of.

"What's going on?" Joel stared at Ben.

"Those cars from the bridge. The ones in the middle." Ben glanced at Joel, then Allie. "They've all been moved to block the northbound lane."

"But we don't have to go that way, so we're okay, right?" Joel swallowed hard.

"Not if they blocked the other bridge, too. They watched us drive in here last night and cut off our escape route. For all we know, the next bridge could have already been blocked off. They just didn't expect us to get off the road and disappear into the woods."

"So...so what does this mean?" Allie put her hand over her mouth.

Ben glared out the window toward the bridge. "We're trapped!"

168

Find out about Bruno Miller's next book by signing up for his newsletter:
http://brunomillerauthor.com/sign-up/

No spam, no junk, just news (sales, freebies, and releases). Scouts honor.

Enjoy the book?
Help the series grow by telling a friend about it
and taking the time to leave a review.

ABOUT THE AUTHOR

BRUNO MILLER is the author of the Dark Road series. He's a military vet who likes to spend his downtime hanging out with his wife and kids, or getting in some range time. He believes in being prepared for any situation.

http://brunomillerauthor.com/

https://www.facebook.com/BrunoMillerAuthor/

28196240R00101

Printed in Poland
by Amazon Fulfillment
Poland Sp. z o.o., Wrocław